UNDERTOW

COASTAL ELITE #2

SAM MARIANO

This is a work of fiction. Names, characters, businesses, places, events
and incidents are either the products of the author's imagination, or used
fictitiously. Any resemblance to actual persons, living or dead, or actual
events is purely coincidental.

Undertow (Coastal Elite, #2) Copyright © 2022 by Sam Mariano

ISBN: 9798844229893

Cover design: Clarise Tan, CT Cover Creations

All rights reserved.

UNDERTOW

SAM MARIANO

For Melissa,

Thank you for all you do.
I appreciate you. <3

EYES STRAIGHT AHEAD. *Just pretend you don't see him.*

It's not unusual for my shoulders and spine to be straight when I'm driving. I've been dancing since I was four years old, so I know the importance of good posture.

Unfortunately, good posture isn't the reason for my straight spine as I drive down the road I live on. Tension is. I can feel it building in my shoulders and gathered in my upper back as I get closer to my driveway.

A place that once brought me feelings of peace and contentment has been tarnished with inky dread. I used to love coming home from work. Now it's like this every time.

A shame, too, since it's such a pretty drive.

The road I live on is lined with similar-looking homes—monuments that the people living inside have fulfilled the elusive American dream.

I'll admit the houses in the neighborhood are very nice.

The people? Not so much.

Especially Brent Hartley and his awful wife, Lisa. If their garage door is even open when I'm driving home, I tense up. Right now, Brent is standing at the edge of his driveway in black shorts and a white T-shirt, a navy blue baseball cap covering most of his short dark hair.

I don't turn my head to let on that I even notice him as I pass, but I can feel his gaze shift in my direction.

Ignoring him even harder, I drive past the next house, then turn left into my own driveway.

My house is a little different from the rest, but it's still a lovely home, and I was so proud to move into it with my daughter. I could never afford a home like the rest on this street. I shouldn't even be able to afford to live near them, but I purchased this empty lot in the coastal town of Baymont, California, many years ago when my daughter was just three years old. I bought it when her father and I were still together, and I had dreams of us being a typical, happy family. Back before I knew what a disappointment he would turn out to be.

The dream home never happened, not while I was with him. Not soon after, either.

At times, I was tempted to sell this plot of land. I desperately needed the money, and I almost caved when the developer that bought up all the land around it offered me close to double what it was worth.

At first, I couldn't understand why he wanted my little plot of land so badly, but then these big, beautiful homes started going up all around it, and I realized the truth. My little plot was a pimple on the face of this lovely, upper-class neighborhood. They wanted to pop me so I'd go away and they could build another beautiful, expensive house.

I didn't sell, though.

When he realized I wouldn't sell, he made me a different offer: they would build me a home just like the others on this street—a stripped-down model, of course—and they would sell it to me at cost so I could afford it. It wouldn't have the interior upgrades and higher-end finishes, but even a base model of a Darington home was more than I could ever dream of.

For years, I'd owned this lot, and finally, I would have a dream home to put on it.

It seemed like a dream come true. I couldn't wait to live in this beautiful, family-friendly neighborhood. It's a safe place, a cul-de-sac, the absolute ideal. My daughter could make friends with the other kids in the neighborhood and go to an amazing school. It would be a great place for us to live.

Boy, was I wrong.

When Brent Hartley and Jayden Todd came walking up my driveway the first time they caught me on my lot, they seemed welcoming, if a little sexist. They wanted to know when my husband would be around since they hadn't seen him yet. When I explained I didn't have a husband, thought bubbles seemed to hang in the air over their heads with a burning question: Then how did you buy a house?

All by my little ole self.

I didn't say that, of course, because I didn't want to start off on the wrong foot.

The developer had asked me not to tell any of the neighbors about the deal he gave me on the house. He didn't want anyone to get jealous or feel ripped off, and I wouldn't want them to feel that way, either. If it mattered enough to him to have a uniform neighborhood that he was willing to build me such a beautiful home at such a reduced price, I could certainly repay the favor by keeping my mouth shut.

I smiled and explained to my new neighbors that I was a single mother of a teenage daughter, and we couldn't wait to move in. We had been renting before, so this was our first home. I didn't explain how I could afford it, and although I could tell they wanted to, they didn't come out and ask.

They didn't seem thrilled for us, but I shrugged it off and went about my day.

It turned out that Jayden lived directly across the street from me. He enjoyed eyeing up my lawn as if he didn't appreciate my leisurely lawn-mowing schedule—or maybe it was that I did it myself. Everyone else on our street has services that come to take care of things like that for them, but not me. I have gardening gloves and a little metal trowel for stubborn weeds, and a mower that I drag out when I need to trim the lawn.

Other than his snobbish behavior, Jayden wasn't much of a problem.

The next time I saw Brent, though, he made it a point

to tell me about a buddy of his who wanted to move into the neighborhood, but unfortunately, all the homes had sold. I nodded sympathetically, a bit impatient for him to leave so I could get back to my herb garden. Then he sprang his reason for stopping by and told me if I ever wanted to sell, I should let him know so he could let his buddy know.

I had no idea why he thought I would want to sell. I let him see my confusion and told him no, my daughter and I were perfectly happy where we were and had no plans to move.

"That's too bad," he said.

I thought it was incredibly rude and didn't even know what to say.

Shortly afterward, I found out from one of the less awful neighbors that Brent's wife had been looking into things, and she found the public record of my purchase—for substantially less than anyone else on this street had paid for their home. She started telling everyone I must have slept with the—married—developer to explain why I got a deal, and she didn't. Inexplicably, despite there being no proof and no reason to believe such a thing, everyone seemed to buy it. I could tell by the snide, sideways looks I started getting.

Since then, the Hartleys, in particular, have been relentless in trying to get me to leave. First, it was their friend who wanted to buy in, then it was Brent's brother and sister-in-law. They don't care who replaces me. They just want me out.

It's bullying, plain and simple. They're the type of people who were obviously popular in high school and didn't get the memo that we've all grown up. Once they decided they wanted me out, that was what was going to happen, and they would terrorize me until they got their way.

They probably figured I would give in easily because I'm soft-spoken and mild-mannered, because I garden and bake, and I teach dance for a living.

It's nothing new, unfortunately. People have underestimated me my whole life.

But it doesn't matter. I'm not going anywhere. No matter how juvenile they are and no matter how miserable they make me. I scrimped and saved every penny I could to buy this home, even at a reduced rate, and I could never afford a nicer, safer place for my daughter and me to live.

Their latest attempts to run me out have been crude and childish. They smashed cheese slices on the side of the house and hurled little green eco-friendly bags of dog poop on my front porch so I would step in it on my way out of the house. The last time I went outside to mow, I had to wear rubber gloves because dozens of open condoms littered my lawn. They weren't used, thank God, but I couldn't mow the lawn until I'd cleaned them all up.

I have a Ring doorbell for security, but everyone on this street does, so they also know the limited visual range and how best to stay out of the way of the camera.

I'm so fed up with their nonsense that I would press charges if I could catch them on camera.

I know they're sitting back and laughing while I'm wasting my time cleaning up after them, but I don't find it a bit funny. Not only are they being mean for no real reason, but they're also eating up time I could be spending with my daughter that I have to spend dealing with their crap instead.

I hit the garage door opener and watch to make sure it rises as I ease down my driveway. Once it's all the way up, I pull in next to my teenage daughter's car and turn off the engine.

I gather my purse and my drinks—coffee *and* a bottle of water, because why choose?—and push my door open to climb out of the car.

"Hey, neighbor."

Dread slithers through me and coils around my tummy. I hold back a sigh and turn to see Brent Hartley standing in the mouth of my open garage like a Cerberus guarding the gates of hell.

There's no escape, he seems to say.

But he's wrong. This is my house, not his, and he's not allowed to be here if I say so.

"Hello, Brent," I say guardedly, pivoting in the tight space between the cars so I can close my door.

He invites himself in, crossing the threshold and walking toward me. "Lovely day, isn't it?"

"It sure is. I really can't talk right now, though. I have to get inside. My daughter's waiting for me to start dinner."

"Oh, yeah? What are you ladies having tonight?"

I turn and look pointedly toward the garage door. "I really don't have time to chat."

"Come on, now. There's no reason to be rude." Ignoring my obvious desire for him to leave, he continues to move closer, his gaze locked on me. "Hey, you know that buddy I was telling you about a long time ago that wanted to move into the neighborhood?"

"Yes."

"Well, things with wife number two didn't work out, and she got the house they ended up moving into. That's how it always works, isn't it?" he says with a smirk that feels vaguely icky.

"I suppose so," I murmur, turning to glance longingly at the garage door leading into my home.

"Anyway, he and wife number three are tying the knot in Aruba next month, and when they get back, they're looking to move into a house. He asked if anything was open in the neighborhood."

"I believe the Burnhams a street over were looking to sell," I tell him.

"Already sold."

"How unfortunate. Well, maybe by the time he gets to wife number four, something will be for sale." I flash him a smile. "Now, if you'll excuse me..."

Rather than leave, he moves forward and plants a hand on the wall to block me from continuing toward the door. "It must be a lot of work keeping up this whole house on your own." His hard gaze meets mine as he leans closer.

"Scary, too. You never know what kind of things can happen to a woman living alone."

I try to back away but only bump into the shelving unit along the wall. "I don't live alone."

"Right," he says with a subtle nod. "*Two* women living alone."

His words and tone fill me with such unease that I lose my manners completely. "Get out of my garage and off my property."

"There's no reason to be rude," he says. "Just being neighborly. Since yours is the only house in the neighborhood without a pool, tell your daughter she can put on a little bikini and swing by my place anytime."

Fury ignites in my veins. "I *said* get off my property."

"Now, Gemma," he says, deliberately condescending, as he grabs my wrist and pushes me back against the shelving unit. "There's no reason to be hysterical."

Just then, the door swings open, and my daughter, Parker, pokes her head out. "Mom?"

My instinct is to tell her to go back into the house, but when Brent's lewd stare turns in her direction, I lose my ability to speak. Fear rushes through me, knocking out my muscles and turning my arms and legs to jelly.

Even though I'm certain he's only doing this in his latest bid to run me out, it doesn't matter.

You don't fuck with my daughter.

"Get out," I growl.

Surprise flits across his features as his gaze shifts back to mine. "Don't worry, I was just leaving." He releases my arm and takes a step back, but my legs still feel as sturdy as Jell-O.

"Remember what I said," he calls as he backs away. "If you change your mind about staying, my buddy will give you a fair price."

Parker stays in the doorway, watching until he's gone.

Finally, her gaze shifts to me, protectiveness etching lines of concern across her pretty face. "Are you all right? You look pale."

"I have had it," I say, each word measured carefully. "I am done with the bullying from these overgrown children. I am done. I have every right to be here, and they have *no* right to treat me this way."

"Agreed," she says. "But without any evidence to prove they're behind all this crap, I don't know what we can do."

I nod slowly. "Well, I'm going to find out." I look over at Parker. "You go to school with a bunch of rich kids. Surely, some have parents who are lawyers. Who is the best lawyer you can think of? The meanest, most aggressive, most successful lawyer around. If one of your classmates got into trouble and their rich mommies and daddies could call anyone to defend them, who would they call?"

"That's easy," Parker says without hesitation. "Satan's dad. Hayden Atwater."

I nod once. "Then I'm going to see Hayden Atwater."

"I'm not sure that's such a good idea. There's no way we can afford him," Parker tells me, but it's too late. I'm already heading back to the car. "Wait, you're going *now?*

You can't go now! Even if we could afford him, you'd need an appointment. You need—Mom, stop. Come inside. Let's think about this first."

"I'm tired of waiting and thinking. It's time for doing. It's time to stop this nonsense once and for all." I get in the car, shut the door, and start the engine. Thankfully, the car is still reasonably cool since I had the air-conditioning on the whole way home, but my skin is hot with anger, so I turn it up a couple of notches.

I glance up to see Parker wide-eyed and waving her arms to get my attention. I check the rearview mirror to make sure Brent didn't come back and I'm about to run him over—*what a pity that would be*—and when I see no one there, I begin to back out.

A text from Parker flashes across my phone screen, but I swipe it away so I can locate the address and phone number of Hayden Atwater's law office. By the time I'm at the end of my road, I have his secretary on the phone checking with him to see if he can take an emergency appointment right away.

Much to my relief, the man says he'll see me.

There have been *many* times over the years our children have gone to school together that I've nearly worked myself up to storming into Hayden Atwater's world and demanding he fix the bully problem in my life.

I just always thought the bully in question would be *his* asshole son, not *my* grown-ass neighbor.

I WAS JUST ABOUT to leave for the day when Sonya told me an angry woman on the phone was demanding to see me right away.

To be honest, I don't have many angry women demanding anything of me. In order for that to happen, you generally need to have *relationships* with women, and I stick to casual encounters. Unless we work together—in which case there will be no romance—I am a one-episode guest star, and I have no interest in reappearing in anyone's life.

I'm not sure what I visualized when I was preparing to meet the angry woman in question, but it was decidedly not the doe-eyed redhead who jingles as she storms gracefully into my office wearing the garb of a *belly dancer*.

It takes a lot to surprise me, but I'm so stunned at the sight of her, I sit behind my desk with my jaw hanging open.

She stops just inside my office, the sheer gauzy fabric

of her purple skirt an endless wave as she moves. It stops and stills when she does. I'm tempted to tell her to keep moving, but while she's standing there, I let my gaze move up over her toned belly to the beaded purple bra encasing her lovely tits.

She looks a bit like a genie.

Are you here to grant me a wish?

The thought crosses my mind as my shock eases, and a faint smile slips into place.

This is a joke. It has to be.

I've been working too hard lately—long hours with no breaks. Sonya has been telling me I need to blow off some steam, and while I never expected her to call in a dancer —*she has worked for me long enough to know I have a soft spot for dancers*—I am impressed with the one she picked out. She's not at all the generically hot Barbie doll blonde with plump lips and seductive eyes that I might have imagined.

No, she's beautiful, but not in a generic way. There's almost an innocence about this woman, which is a ridiculous thought to have given she's probably close to thirty.

Maybe it's because she's standing there looking like *I Dream of Jeannie.*

I hope she calls me master.

I smirk at the thought, folding my hands over my abdomen and leaning back in my leather office chair, waiting for the show to start.

Since the dancer seems to be waiting for me to say

something, I play along. "What can I do for you today, Miss...?"

"Cane," she provides, and even her voice is lovely. "Gemma Cane."

Gemma Cane.

Sweet like a stick of peppermint candy.

That has to be made up. Hell of a stage name, though.

Her skirts sway like ocean waves as she moves closer. "I'm having a problem with my neighbor."

"Oh, yeah? Is her lamp too close to yours?"

A frown flickers across her face. "What? No, it's not a female neighbor, it's—well, he's married, somehow. I can't imagine the desperation one would have to feel to marry a man like that, but I suppose she's cut from the same cloth. I don't like her, either," she informs me.

I nod patiently, waiting for this bit to end and for her to dance her pretty little ass over here and sit on my lap.

"It's the husband. He's... well, forgive my language, but he's a real bastard."

I nod, trying to skip ahead to the good part. "Ah, so you need a knight in shining armor to rescue you? I'm afraid you've come to the wrong place, sweetheart." This is taking up too much of my time, so I pat my thigh to let her know I want to move things along. "Then again, who knows? Maybe if you're really sweet, I can be persuaded."

Her mouth forms a little O of shock, her big brown eyes impossibly going even wider. "If you're insinuating what I think you are, that—that is... incredibly inappropriate."

I'm ready to get even more inappropriate.

I eye her tits, looking for her nipples beneath the heavy beading. "Feigned outrage doesn't do it for me," I tell her, my tone a bit bored. "Come over here and try something else."

I swear to God, she's near fainting. I wish she'd give up the act. I'm interested in her, but not this reluctance bit. I want to see her move, then have her on my lap so I can tug that beaded bra down and take the peaks of her lovely tits in my mouth. I want to know how she tastes.

"I..." She is at a complete loss. Since my gaze is on her chest, she glances down, and when she does, she appears to be as shocked as I was when she walked in. Clutching her breasts and gasping, she looks up at me like a deer in headlights. "Oh my god, I'm still in my work clothes."

Her work clothes?

Is this still part of the act?

"Where do you work?" I ask cautiously, hoping it is.

"A dance school. I'm—I'm a dance teacher." Horrified, her gaze shifts to mine again. "Oh my god, you thought I was a... different kind of dancer."

I'm beginning to fear this is a real appointment and not some sexy setup from my well-meaning assistant.

"You're not here to dance for me," I say slowly.

She shakes her head, no longer looking angry, just deeply embarrassed.

Well, that's damn disappointing.

Damn disappointing.

I don't know what I was looking forward to more,

seeing her dance for me or feeling the weight of her body on my lap before she started lavishing attention on my cock.

I've already got a taste for her now, and she's telling me she's not on the menu?

"I'm so sorry for the confusion," she says.

"So am I," I answer dryly.

"My summer session is wrapping up, and we're rehearsing every day for their recital this weekend. I usually wear regular activewear and just maybe a hip scarf to teach classes, but with it being rehearsal week..." She gives up covering her breasts, and stacks her hands over her tummy. "Well, I guess now I'm the inappropriate one."

Now that she's gentled, I find myself liking her again. I mean, I wanted her tits in my mouth whether I liked her or not, but she has a sweetness that appeals to me beyond that surface level. "You don't have to cover up. I'll stop requesting lap dances now that I know you're an actual client."

Her cheeks flush a bit, and she smiles, shyly avoiding my gaze. "Well, potential client. My daughter tells me you might be outside my price range, but I'm willing to splurge if you can make this problem go away. I was hoping for a consultation and an idea of exactly what it would cost to have your help. I don't even know what I need, to be honest. Maybe a 'cease and desist being a giant douchebag' letter? Is that a thing?"

I find the idea of anyone being a douchebag to her annoying. She seems perfectly nice. What's this neighbor's problem? "Tell me a little more about the conflict, and I'll see what I can do to help."

"Well, my neighbor is a terrible human being. He has been harassing me for a while, trying to chase me out of the neighborhood. I haven't done anything to him, but he found out I paid less for my house than anyone else in the neighborhood paid for theirs because I already owned the land and the developer cut me a deal. I can't prove that he's behind them, but there have been so many juvenile, mean-spirited pranks. Dog poop on the front porch, open condoms all over my lawn. They smashed cheese on the side of my house."

My eyebrows rise. "He smashed *cheese* on the side of your house? Is your neighbor a twelve-year-old?"

Impossibly, her already enormous eyes widen. "Right? So immature. And I've been dealing with their crap since we moved in, but today, he crossed the line. He made comments and lewd insinuations about my daughter, and I will not stand for that."

I scowl, sitting forward and grabbing a pen and paper to take notes. "How old is your daughter?"

"She just turned eighteen in June."

My gaze flickers to her, surprised. "You have an eighteen-year-old?"

A smile flickers across her face. "Dancing keeps me young." She misses a beat, then adds, "And I got pregnant at seventeen."

The mention of getting pregnant stirs thoughts of how a woman *gets* pregnant, and my thoughts regarding her were already far from pure. "Has your husband tried talking to him?"

"I don't have a husband. It's just my daughter and me."

"No husband, huh?" I murmur, watching her. "Boyfriend?"

"Um, no. There's no man available to speak with him. I actually think that's part of why he keeps picking on me. My neighbor strikes me as quite sexist, and he thinks he can pick on me because..."

"There's no one to stop him. He probably wants to fuck you."

Her eyes widen at the audacity of my suggestion. "He's married."

"And...?"

She frowns, but then it eases. "Well, he *is* an asshole, so I suppose that doesn't necessarily rule out his wanting to... Regardless, I don't care what he wants. *I* want the harassment to stop."

I've heard all I need to hear. As soon as she told me there was no husband or boyfriend in the way, I made up my mind that *I'm* going to fuck her—and the sooner, the better, so it's time to close this deal so we can move on.

"All right, Gemma Cane. I would be happy to help you with your neighbor problem."

She's so pretty when she smiles. Gazing at me like I'm the answer to all her prayers, she says, "You will?"

I nod, already hating my next words since I know they'll wipe that smile off her face. "Absolutely. Before we go any further, though, I should tell you I charge $1,400 an hour, and we bill in fifteen-minute chunks. So, as soon as you stormed into my office in your jingly little outfit, you owed me $350."

As I predicted, her smile falls. "Uh, fourteen... wow. Per hour. That's, um, that seems like quite a lot of money."

"It is."

"You must be really good."

I smile. "I am."

"I don't... So—so you don't do like a free consultation or anything?"

I lean back in my chair and shake my head. "They say if you're good at something, never do it for free, and we just covered that, didn't we?"

"Yeah, I guess we did." She looks down, tucking a chunk of ginger hair behind her ear. "Unfortunately, it seems my daughter was right. That's definitely outside our budget."

I knew it would be, so I don't feign surprise. I let her be uncomfortable for a few seconds to see what she does.

I've made my interest in her pretty clear. Some part of me is curious if she'll "joke" about paying another way to see if I bite.

Another part hopes she doesn't.

It's where we're heading, but I don't want it to be her idea.

"I guess there's no point in discussing this any further, then," she says, clearly disappointed. "I should probably go figure out billing with your receptionist before the bill gets even bigger. Do you take payments? Or I have a credit card. I suppose I can just…"

"You still have a few minutes left," I tell her. "You can at least give me your neighbor's information so I can start looking into him."

"Why? I can barely pay for the consultation. I certainly can't afford to hire you."

"What if you could?"

"I can't."

"I'll make you a deal," I say, watching her closely. "We can finish up your consultation—however long it takes—and I'll scrap the bill altogether if you agree to meet me later for a drink."

Her wide eyes shoot to my face. "A drink?"

I nod. "Cold things, come in a glass, often with ice cubes."

She rolls her eyes lightly but appears a bit nervous. "I know what a drink is. I just don't think I should have one with you."

My brow furrows. "Why not?"

Her gaze drops. I can tell she's thinking about it, but she's reluctant. "I just don't think it's a good idea. And it's pointless—I can't hire you."

"But you can save yourself $350," I counter. "Plus, once you've consulted with me, should it come to that, he won't be able to hire me to represent *him*. Conflict of interest; I'm already privy to too many details about your side of the case. Whether you hire me or not, I guarantee you don't want me on *his* side of the courtroom."

This should be a no-brainer. I've never had to bribe a woman to have a drink with me before, and the deal is even sweeter for her. She can literally save hundreds of dollars just by agreeing to have one drink with me.

Well, I'm sure it won't be one drink, but who cares? I'm paying.

Just in case, by some slim chance, that's why she isn't jumping at my offer, I tell her with feigned solemnity, "I'll even pay for the drinks."

She smiles but doesn't look at me. "It isn't that. I just... I can't have a drink with you. I'm sorry."

"Not even if it saves you $350?"

She shakes her head, almost regretfully.

I frown, confused.

That's fucking insane.

"Why?" I demand.

Rather than answer me, she says, "I've wasted enough of your time. I think I'll just look into filing a restraining order instead."

"Do you not drink? We can do dinner instead."

"No, thank you."

I've never been turned down so relentlessly before, and I'm not sure what to do with it.

I think about offering more, but I don't like to make desperate moves. Hell, no woman has ever had me in a position where I'd even *consider* it, but I don't understand why she's so adamantly disinterested in going out with me —and I'm *very* adamantly interested in going out with *her*.

She turns to go back out to reception to ask about a

payment plan or charge a fucking credit card she'll probably spend months paying off. All because she'd rather pay than spend a single evening in my company.

I should be insulted. I am a little, but more than that, I'm confused.

"Your neighbor. Tell me his name."

She turns back to look at me over her shoulder. "Why?"

"Just do it."

She's startled by the command, but rather than tell me to go to hell, she says, "Brent Hartley. His wife's name is Lisa."

"Thank you."

She nods, trying not to be rude, but also trying to drop my gaze like she's afraid to look at me for too long.

I guess I have to release her.

I don't want to, but that doesn't make any sense, so I nod back.

Her gaze leaves mine immediately, and she flees my office without another word.

My phone vibrates on my desk, but I don't look at it until Gemma is out of sight.

It's a text from my housekeeper telling me the salmon she was about to prepare for dinner is unexpectedly bad, and we'll have to change tonight's menu.

I grab the phone and shoot a quick text back, telling her I won't be home for dinner, after all. She can just make something for Landon.

Then I slide the phone across the desk and turn my attention to my computer.

Clearly, Gemma's going to need a little more convincing.

I should probably let it go, but I've never been known to take no for an answer.

Let's see what I can find out about Brent Hartley before I take Gemma Cane out for that drink.

WHEN REHEARSAL WRAPS up for the day, Nancy continues to struggle with her timing. Since it's Friday and we're out of official rehearsal time, I offer to stay a little late and work with her on perfecting her moves.

Ordinarily, I'd want to get home to Parker, and I do, but Nancy isn't like my other belly dancing students who are mostly taking the class as a fun workout. She's an older lady who always wanted to learn to belly dance when she was younger, but she was too self-conscious about showing her tummy. After surviving cancer, she realized there are plenty of things to be afraid of, but a bare stomach isn't one of them. She's so proud of herself for finally putting herself out there and having fun without worrying what people think about her. She even has her grown son and his wife and kids coming to watch her, so she wants to be perfect at the recital.

I text Parker that I'll be working late and stay to practice with Nancy until she finally nails the rhythm. When we stop for a water break before she leaves, she gives me a hug and thanks me.

"You're gonna knock 'em dead, girl," I assure her, smiling as I uncap my water bottle to take a drink.

She beams at me as she makes her way over to grab her purse. "Thank you for staying late, honey. You didn't have to do that."

"It was fun," I assure her with a smile. "I'm so glad you took my class this summer."

"So am I," she says, shimmying her hips and making me laugh.

When Nancy leaves, I turn off all the lights and prepare to leave as well. I grab my phone and see I have several missed texts from Parker, so I swipe the screen and open the message chain to see what I've missed.

Mostly there are just texts of her asking when I'm coming home, but she must be getting hungry because the messages are getting hilariously weird. She sent me individual pictures of ham and slices of cheese with sad faces drawn on in purple marker in markup mode, then she sent three sobbing emojis with the added caption, "Me because I don't have jamón y queso in my tummy right now."

I grin and text back, "I'm sorry! Nancy and I JUST finished. Mommy is on the way to save the day right now!"

She sends back party emojis instantaneously, and I smile, slipping the phone into my purse and drawing out my keys.

Movement in the dark auditorium makes my heart drop and wipes the smile right off my face. I clutch my car keys, my heart stuttering, and try to remember what I'm supposed to do if I'm accosted in the dark by a stranger.

There shouldn't be anyone else here. I stayed late with Nancy, but she left, and everyone else went home when rehearsal ended.

Before I can have a full-blown heart attack, the man moves out of the shadows, and I realize it's not a stranger at all—well, not a *total* stranger.

It's Hayden Atwater.

He looks *devastatingly* handsome in his expensive three-piece suit, stepping out of the shadows like some-body's nightmare.

My insides flutter, but I need him to leave, and I guess before that, I need to know what the hell he's doing here.

"This is a closed rehearsal," I say with a frown, casting a confused look at the row he just emerged from.

Was he sitting there watching me?

"Rehearsal ended"—he checks his Rolex—"about an hour ago. Do you often stay late to help little old ladies learn how to rock their hips?"

My cheeks flush, and I look down at my water bottle to avoid looking at him. "No, not usually. I don't generally have elderly ladies in my belly dancing class, or any of my classes, really." Rather than continue to explain myself to him, I ask, "Why are you here?"

"Wanted to see you dance. You ripped me off yesterday."

A short laugh bursts out of me. "I ripped *you* off? You ogled me and did nothing, and I had to pay *you* $350."

"You didn't have to," he reminds me. "I offered to take you out for a drink and wipe the slate clean."

He moves toward me, and I find myself taking a step back. Rationally, I know he's no predator. He's a lawyer, for heaven's sake.

But he did sneak into my closed rehearsal to watch me dance, and now we're completely alone, and...

He needs to leave.

Clearing my throat, I attempt a firm tone and tell him, "I believe we concluded our business yesterday, and I really have to be getting home to my daughter, so if you'll excuse me..."

He doesn't stop moving toward me, and I don't stop retreating.

"This is very inappropriate," I tell him as I'm forced to continue backing up.

His lips tug up in a smirk, amusement sparking in his dark eyes. They're the color of the ocean at night. "You use that word a lot."

"Only when I'm around you."

His gaze rakes over me. "Turquoise today, huh? I like it."

"Why are you stalking me?" I demand since he's still advancing on me.

"Why are you letting me?" he returns, cocking an eyebrow.

I'm right up against the stage now. I can't retreat any farther, so I stop, jutting my chin up and meeting his gaze. "I'm not letting you. I just can't seem to stop you."

He stops too, but he's right on top of me. Far too close. His nearness makes my heart hammer in my chest.

"I think I'm beginning to understand why your neighbor loves tormenting you," he states.

Narrowing my eyes, I say, "You would sympathize with the *asshole* in this scenario."

He smiles at my insult as though he finds me adorable. "I didn't say I sympathized with him, just that I understood. There's a difference between empathy and sympathy."

"I'm aware of that," I mutter.

"I want to take you out for a drink," he states.

"While I *empathize* with you wanting that," I tell him, lightly mocking, "I am not going anywhere with you, least of all for a drink."

"Why are you so determined not to go out with me?"

"Has it occurred to you that maybe I just don't like you?"

"No," he says plainly.

I roll my eyes in disgust.

"I know you're attracted to me. I make you nervous."

"Do you think every woman you make nervous must be attracted to you? Because I'm afraid I have some bad news..."

"I don't ordinarily spend time with women I make nervous. I'm making an exception for you."

"How delightful for me."

He grins. "Isn't it? Now, are you going home to change

first, or do you want to just wear your little scarves to the bar? We can make it a tradition."

I shake my head. Since he isn't advancing on me anymore, I brush past him and walk quickly toward the exit. "I already told you, the answer is no. It's still no. It will always be no. I also told you my daughter is waiting on me to start dinner, so why you think there's even a *chance* I'll go out with you right now—"

"Tell her something came up. I'll order her a pizza," he offers.

"I am not blowing off my daughter to go out for a drink I don't want with *you*."

"Ouch." He grabs at his heart, if he even has one. "You wound me, Gemma Cane."

Ignoring him, I shove open the auditorium doors and make my way out without holding the door for him. Maybe that'll show him I mean business.

He follows me. "I think I should warn you, the last time a woman made me work this hard to go out with her, I married her."

I spin around, eyes wide. He has me so discombobulated that I momentarily forget what I once knew about him. "You're *married*? You *are* an asshole."

He shakes his head, his expression changing. A granite shield slips into place, as if masking old pain he doesn't want me to see. "Widowed."

My heart stops. My chest fills up with something tight and painful. "Oh. Oh, my god. I knew that. I'm so sorry."

The details are murky, but I remember all the bullying from Hayden's son started when Parker was in middle school, right after his mother died. Sympathy for what that poor little boy must have been going through was the only reason I didn't charge into a grieving Hayden Atwater's office back then and demand he stop his son from being an asshole to my daughter.

That sympathy worked against me then—it has been years, and his awful son still torments my daughter—so I don't make the mistake of letting it happen again.

"Well, I'm very sorry for your loss, but don't think my sympathy changes my answer."

"I would never exploit my wife's death to charm a woman, Miss Cane, even one as lovely as you." My face heats, but he gracefully leaps to the next topic, somehow in a way that doesn't feel all that strange. "Don't get me wrong, you're still going out with me, just not for that reason. I have the perfect place in mind. I think you'll like it."

"Based on all you know about me?" I mutter.

As if he didn't even hear me, he plods on. "I guess if you're committed to having dinner with your daughter tonight, we can go out afterward. That gives you time to change out of your costume, anyway." His gaze rakes over me before returning to my face. "How does 8:30 sound? I'll pick you up."

I stare up at him, wide-eyed. "You are relentless."

He smiles. "I know. Makes me a damn good attorney."

"I've told you no a thousand times. I shouldn't have to say it again."

"Why don't you try a different answer? One I'll like better."

I sigh, exiting the dance school and heading for my car. "Why don't *you* try asking out a woman who actually wants to go out with you? You're handsome, and you charge $1,400 an hour, so you're clearly not struggling to pay the bills. Surely this town is full of women tripping all over themselves for your attention."

"Eh, too easy. I want you."

I know he only means he wants to have a drink with me, but his wording makes my stomach drop. I've never had a man boldly tell me that he wants me before.

We've made it to my car, but he's still following me. The only thing left to do is get in and drive away, but since the man won't go away, I turn back to face him.

"I don't date," I say. Maybe if I give more of an explanation, he'll give up. "This is my daughter's last year before she leaves for college, and I want to focus all of my free time on her right now. I have the rest of my life to waste on relationships that aren't going anywhere. I've chosen to sit it out this year. If you want a rain check, I'll give you one," I offer, knowing he'll never remember he wanted to go out with me in a year's time.

He's scowling, displeased by my explanation. "You can't go out with me because you're not dating this year?"

"Correct."

"That's absurd. Tell me the real reason."

"That *is* the real reason."

"No." He shakes his head. "You were very adamant

about not wanting to go out with *me*, specifically. If your dating fast was the real reason, you would've mentioned it right away."

I stare at him. "Maybe I didn't think I owed you an explanation for why I didn't want to go out with you."

"Well, you were wrong."

My eyes narrow with dislike before I can stop them. Finally, unlocking my car door and opening it, I say, "As lovely as this has been, I'm going home."

He grabs my car door, letting me get in but preventing me from closing it. "What makes you think it isn't going anywhere?"

I glance up at him. "What?"

"You said you have the rest of your life to go on dates that aren't going anywhere, that's why you don't think dating is a thing worth doing while your daughter still lives at home."

"I did."

"Why such a dour outlook on dating?" he asks.

"I don't have a dour outlook on dating." I tug at the door, but he doesn't release it, so I shoot him a dirty look. "I have a dour outlook on dating *you*."

His eyebrows rise. "Why?"

I could give him plenty of reasons. He's pushy and annoying, he doesn't listen to me when I speak, and I've never found frustrating men particularly charming.

But the real answer is profoundly uncomfortable. Even if it's the truth, I don't relish the idea of insulting someone's child.

Wanting to be free of this interaction rather than have to do that, I give my door another tug. "Let go."

"Not until you tell me why you don't like me."

"It isn't you I don't like," I snap, surprised by my own answer.

I don't dislike him?

That doesn't seem right.

Since my answer doesn't make sense and he's still frowning, I decide to pound the nail in the coffin of his romantic interest in me. "I don't like your son."

He blinks like that's the absolute last guess he ever would have made. "My *son?*"

I nod, feeling my face heat. Even though my opinion is completely warranted, I feel like a witch saying it.

But surely now he sees. There's no point whatsoever in spending time with someone who doesn't like your child. There's no future in it.

I had a first date planned with a man once. He came to pick me up, and when Parker ran over to give me a hug and kiss before I left, I caught a look of utter disdain pass across his face. When pressed, he said he wasn't a big fan of kids.

I didn't bother going on the date. What would have been the point? Parker wasn't going anywhere, and if he wasn't willing to love her like I did, he had no business being in my life.

I don't see myself *ever* liking Landon Atwater, so his father could be the man of my dreams and it still wouldn't work.

Understandably confused, he asks, "What does my son have to do with anything?"

"My daughter and your son go to school together."

"Yes, you mentioned that."

"My daughter is Parker Johansson," I tell him since he probably would have expected my last name to match my daughter's, and he hadn't heard any mention of Parker Cane.

Not so much as a hint of recognition registers on his face.

I frown, a little insulted on Parker's behalf.

He's never even mentioned her?

That seems wrong, but Hayden is clearly clueless when it comes to the relationship between our children.

I don't see how. I've heard so much about Landon Atwater over the years, I feel like I know the little jerk even though we've never met.

"Is that name supposed to mean something to me?" he asks.

"Yes," I snap. "Your asshole son has bullied my daughter since *middle school*. I assumed you knew and just didn't care how your son behaved, but now I'm thinking you actually aren't even aware of what goes on with him."

"I'm a very busy man, and Landon has a lot of friends," he says a touch dismissively. "I can't possibly keep up with the goings-on regarding his social life."

"Well, they are *not* friends," I tell him. "He's mean to

her, and I obviously can't date someone whose son is mean to my daughter."

"Maybe he likes her," Hayden suggests, not remotely alarmed or surprised to hear that his son is a bully.

"Nuh-uh, no. We do not entertain the narrative that if a boy is mean to you, that means he likes you."

"Entertain it or don't, but it's probably the truth."

I stare at him, letting him see how unimpressed I am.

"I'll talk to him," he says since the dismissive route didn't get him far. "I'll tell him to stop picking on her."

"I would appreciate that," I say, slightly mollified. At least he isn't one of those parents who knows what a jerk their kid is but just doesn't care.

"Now, with that out of the way, how about that drink?"

I sigh, shaking my head at him. "You don't give up, do you?"

"Not when I want something. Sorry," he says, though he doesn't look at all sorry.

I definitely *shouldn't* go out with him. There's no question it's a bad idea, and I really am taking the year off dating so I can focus on Parker.

But I can't remember the last time I went out on a nice date, and I do have a feeling I would have a good time with him. I also have a feeling if I keep telling him no, I'll keep seeing him until he wears me out and gets a yes.

I suppose one little drink couldn't cause any real harm.

"Make it 9:30," I say.

Victory glints in his eyes as he smiles down at me. "Perfect. I'll pick you up."

"Don't you need my address?"

"Already have it."

I roll my eyes playfully. "Stalker."

"Hey, if you can drive me to stalking, you should feel pretty damn proud of yourself. I usually can't be bothered to answer a text."

I'm not sure he should admit that, but in a way it's comforting. It verifies what I already thought—that taking me out for this drink is only appealing to him because I keep turning him down. As soon as he takes me out and realizes I'm a boring mom and he could be out with a gorgeous, college-aged beach bunny instead, he'll lose interest and leave me alone.

I don't know how this keeps happening to me, but at least *this* relentless pursuer is handsome and unmarried.

WHEN I DRIVE HOME TONIGHT, the Hartley garage is open, but I don't see Brent's car.

As soon as I get my car in my garage, I lower the door anyway, just in case.

I'm still uneasy until I get in the house and see Parker sitting at the island, reading a book.

"One minute," she says without looking up. "They just kissed and there was a scene break, but it's only a few paragraphs, and I want to finish the chapter. You know I hate stopping before a chapter ends."

I crack a smile, dropping my bag on the counter beside the fridge. "I thought you were over here wasting away."

"I was, but you took so long I decided to start my new book, and now here we are." She ignores me, focusing her attention on her story while I move around the kitchen gathering ingredients and cooking supplies.

Even though I had the whole drive home, I haven't decided whether I'll tell Parker who I'm going out with tonight. There probably isn't a reason to. We're only going for a drink. It's not like we'll ever go out again.

I won't lie to her, but maybe I'll be vague and just tell her I'm having a drink with a friend.

Given how immersed she is in her new story, she probably won't even ask questions. She'll want to be free to read her book tonight, so she won't be disappointed I'll be out.

This worked out kind of perfectly.

Once Parker finishes her page, she closes the book and comes over to help me make the ham and cheese rolls we picked out for tonight's dinner. I feel guilty for being distracted the whole time, but I can't seem to get my mind off my nighttime plans.

I can't actually remember the last date I went on. Not only because it has been a long time, but because years of aimless dates have run together.

Was it Dev, the cheap guy who invited me out for drinks and then refused to actually order anything but water so I would have to pay for my own? Was it the guy with the greaser hair-do who had no opinions about anything and then told me during dinner that his last girlfriend had been married, but hey, he doesn't judge? Could've been the bankrupt divorced dad whose idea of a date was me coming over to his place to watch a football game on TV and trying to maul me while his two-year-old took a nap. Maybe it was Brad, the doctor I had been excited about because surely a doctor would be an intelligent conversationalist at the very least. But no. He was boring and a bad kisser.

Actually, I think it might have been him. That date left a sour taste in my mouth—literally—and I felt so dejected when I got home that night, I decided to take a hiatus from dating altogether.

It feels wrong to even include Hayden in the same group as those men for reasons I can't explain.

It's completely possible he'll turn out to be a total asshole. Even if he isn't, it can't go anywhere, so I shouldn't get my hopes up.

It will be nice to go out, though.

Maybe.

I find myself watching the clock, keeping track of how long I have to get ready as Parker and I cook and then eat. She tells me about her book, and I tell her about Nancy, but I don't mention Hayden, and it's difficult to feel like I'm not lying to her.

It feels a little like betrayal going out with the father of the enemy, though.

That probably means I shouldn't go, but I suppose it's too late to back out now. I don't even have his cell phone number to text him and tell him I changed my mind.

I don't know what to wear. I stand in my small walk-in closet looking at everything I own, but I don't actually know where we're going. He asked me out for a drink, so probably a bar, but what kind? A quiet wine bar with other adults where we will have a nice, quiet conversation?

A lively club packed full of beautiful, writhing bodies and scarcely a soul over thirty?

God, I hope it's not a place like that. I didn't like clubs when I was in my early twenties, so I certainly don't want to step foot in one now.

My closet is arranged by color, but I'm grabbing hangers from every section and hauling them to the bed. There's a green dress, a blue dress, and even a white. High neck, strapless, maybe a halter?

Parker walks by on the way to her bedroom, but she stops dead in her tracks, her eyes widening as she looks at the mess on my ordinarily pristine bed.

"What is going on in here?" she asks slowly.

I'm still in a towel. I took a shower and blew out my hair, but I feel woefully unprepared to dress myself.

"I don't know what to wear."

She eyes me uncertainly. "To grab a drink with a friend?"

"Yes. I don't know where we're going, so I'm not sure how I should dress. I don't want to be overdressed. Or underdressed."

A knowing smile plays around her lips, and she teases, "Is this a male friend?"

I shoo her away. "Go read your book."

She grins but doesn't give me a hard time. Eyeing the mess of clothes on my bed, she walks around to the side I'm standing on. She must not see what she's looking for because she turns and heads for my closet. "What about the red lace one with three-quarter sleeves?"

That one has a high neck, but it's lacy and classy. I love that dress, but I think I want something more overtly sexy. A lower neckline.

Why?

I shove the thought away and grab a navy blue strapless one. I look at it, but my displeasure shows on my face.

"All right, what about a two-piece ensemble?" Parker suggests, seeing the difference in the dress she picked out and the one I did. "Your short black skirt that makes your legs look like they go on for days. You could pair it with— Oh! I've got it." She snatches a sparkly navy blazer from the black section, then heads back into my bedroom and grabs the skirt and a black silk blouse I tossed on the bed. "This," she says, handing the pieces to me. "This outfit with your strappy, black suede heels."

I drape it across the bed and look at the outfit she picked out for me. It's actually kind of perfect. If I'm overdressed, I can take off the blazer and I won't be anymore.

"What would I do without you?" I ask rhetorically.

"You're welcome," she says, fleeing my room so she can get back to reading. "Have fun on your date," she calls playfully before disappearing down the hall.

"It's not a date," I murmur, but she's already gone so I'm only lying to myself.

When the royal blue Maserati that obviously belongs to Hayden Atwater pulls into my driveway, I rush out the door like a teenager reluctant to let her parents meet a date she knows they'll disapprove of.

Parker is upstairs in her room, but I don't want him to come to the door and risk her getting curious.

My heels click against the concrete driveway as I hurry around to the passenger side. I flash him a smile as I open the door and slide in. "Hello, again."

"Long time no see," he says lightly, watching me smooth down the back of my skirt and drop into the two-tone leather seat. "You seem like you're in a hurry. You must have missed me."

I shoot him a look and roll my eyes, but I *am* in a hurry and have to resist the urge to follow it up with, "Now go, go, go!"

Hayden doesn't hurry, though. If anything, I think my impatience slows him down. Clearly, he's a man who does things on his own schedule.

His gaze rakes over me appreciatively. "You look beautiful."

"Thank you," I say a bit shyly, tucking my hair behind my ear and looking at him in his black T-shirt and charcoal gray dinner jacket. Black slacks stretch across his muscular thighs, and my face warms as my gaze returns to his. "You look very handsome yourself."

As he backs out of the driveway, I glance at the house to make sure it's secure. Grabbing my phone out of my little navy blue purse, I text Parker and tell her I locked up on the way out and I have my keys. "If the doorbell rings, ignore it. Do not unlock or open the door to anyone while I'm out."

Right as I push send, Hayden questions, "Something pressing going on over there?"

I glance over at him. "Sorry, I was just texting Parker to remind her not to answer the door while I'm out. I don't *think* my neighbor is actually dangerous, but since he's escalating his attempts to run me out, I'm just not willing to take any chances."

His brow furrows with concern. "You're that worried about him?"

I shrug, uncomfortable actually saying it out loud. "I feel a little silly about it, but he was very threatening the last time he cornered me in my garage. He grabbed my arm and pushed me back against the shelving unit. I don't know what would have happened if Parker hadn't opened the door, but—" I freeze in horror as he cuts the wheel and turns into the Hartley driveway. "What are you doing?"

"Something impulsive."

"Let's not," I say, my conflict-averse tendencies rearing their heads. "I was very clear that I wanted to send a strongly worded letter, not—" He ignores me, leaving the car running and climbing out of it. "Hayden," I whisper urgently, opening my door and hastily following after him.

I don't know if I'm supposed to follow or stay in the car. I feel so awkward I could die either way.

I arrive on the porch just in time to see Hayden ring the doorbell. It's too late to turn back now, but interactions like these are literally the stuff my nightmares are made of.

Lisa comes to the door. At first, she looks pleasantly surprised to see a handsome man on her doorstep, but her expression changes swiftly when she sees me just behind him.

"How can I help you?" she asks uncertainly.

"I'm here to see Brent," Hayden informs her. "Is he home?"

She realizes he must be here on my behalf, so her attitude resurfaces. "No, I'm afraid he's out."

"Ah." Hayden nods. "Well, in that case, could you do me a favor? Tell your husband that the next time he corners my girlfriend on her property and puts his hands on her, the assault charges she's going to file against him will be the *least* of his problems. And I've installed extra cameras to ensure her safety, so next time, she'll also have video evidence."

Lisa's jaw falls open.

Hayden turns around without another word and heads back to his car.

Her gaze hits mine, her eyes wide with rage.

Without a word, I also turn around and scamper after my date.

"Hey," Lisa calls belligerently, but neither of us even pauses.

We get right back in the Maserati, then Hayden backs out of the driveway, and it's over.

Well, for us.

I can't bite back a little smile. "He's probably going to have a bad night."

Hayden looks over at me and smirks. "I hope so."

"I hope that doesn't make things worse," I murmur since there obviously *are* no cameras and Hayden isn't actually my boyfriend. The implication that I have a protector now was nice, but since I don't, it could backfire. He could come at me even harder now.

"It could go either way. If he's picking on you because he perceives you to be weaker and unable to defend yourself against him, knowing you have someone proactive in your corner should be enough to shake him. The old adage of 'once you stand up to a bully, the bullying stops' coming into play. Of course, that wouldn't work with an asshole like me. I'm the sort to see it through, but I also don't go after easy targets. Only cowards do that."

"I'm not weak," I murmur, looking down at my purse on my lap.

I feel Hayden's gaze shift to me. "I didn't mean to imply that you're weak, Gemma. Only that a certain kind of asshole might think that because you have a gentle nature. Have you ever heard the concept of Maslow's hammer? That when the only tool you have is a hammer, everything looks like a nail? Some people don't know any other way, so they assume theirs—in this case, being an asshole—is the one right way, and everyone else is wrong. They lack the empathy or intelligence to understand things outside of their own experience, so they ridicule it instead. I'm far from gentle, but I know it takes guts and determination to remain that way in the world we live in, so I certainly don't agree with that small-minded opinion."

I bite down on my bottom lip, trying to suppress my smile so it doesn't get too big. "Wow, two minutes into this date, and you've already defended my honor twice and quoted psychological philosophy at me. Are you trying to win an award or something?"

"Or something," he murmurs playfully, his eyes glinting with mischief.

I'm pretty sure his implication is purely playful, but it still makes my face warm.

I don't have sex on first dates. I'm extremely slow to warm up. Henry Cavill could don Superman's cape mid-date and save a kitten from a tree, and I still wouldn't give him more than a hug and a lingering kiss.

Unless someone makes it past casual dating to being my actual boyfriend, there's little chance I'm sleeping with him.

But if I *did* sleep with men on first—*and only*—dates? I think I'd probably sleep with Hayden Atwater.

HE TAKES me to a bar I've never been to before—a place called Underworld located right on the beach.

From the looks of it, it's a hotel bar with a little walkway connecting the hotel lobby and the bar area down by the beach. The bar has its own separate parking lot, though, and is clearly an independent destination.

The salty beach air fills my senses as I step out of the car and walk around to join Hayden. I take his hand, but I'm not sure why. I like affection with boyfriends, of course, but I'm not terribly bold, and I would never just grab the hand of a man I barely know on a first date.

I do, though. He looks down at our joined hands but doesn't seem to mind.

I shouldn't be holding his hand.

I can't shake the thought as we head toward the entrance to the bar. I keep wanting to react to him like I would an actual date that I'm giving a real chance, but this was never supposed to be that. It doesn't even matter if I like him. I already know this can't go anywhere, so there's no point.

I look up at the glowing blue sign with three scary-looking black dogs peeking over the name 'Underworld.'

"Welcoming," I say wryly.

He glances up. I get the impression he comes here so often, he hasn't even noticed the sign in a while. "Oh, yeah. The owner's dramatic."

"You sound familiar."

"I hope so. He's my brother." He opens the door for me.

I thank him as I step inside. "You have a brother?"

"A couple," he answers wryly. "I'm one of six kids."

My eyes widen. "*Six* kids? Your mom and dad must have really liked each other."

He laughs, shaking his head. "Actually, no. My father is a decidedly unpleasant man. He was worse when he was younger. His rage could just swallow you up." He puts a hand on the small of my back and guides me through a small crowd lingering near the entry doors. "They're divorced now, but I guess when she was younger, my mom must have been really into his toxicity."

"Happens to the best of us," I say wryly.

"What about you?" he asks, glancing over at me. "Any siblings?"

I shake my head. "Only child. My parents also divorced, but my father passed when I was a teenager. Mom remarried, and they live in Florida now, so we don't see them much."

He nods. "So the toxic asshole in your life..."

"Parker's father. He was a liar, a cheat, and he was gaslighting me long before I knew what gaslighting was. We were on-again, off-again forever, but it's hard when you have a kid together and can't really break away. I finally realized Parker and I could never have anything good as long as I let him stick around, so I cut it off." He nods like he understands, so I ask carefully, "What about your wife? Was your marriage a good one?"

"A great one. Mostly because of her. We married young, so I didn't know what the hell I was doing. She didn't either, but she figured it out." He smiles faintly.

The noise picks up a little once we're in the heart of the bar. A black bar with a blue glow is the focal point in the center of the room, and everything else unfolds around it. The seats at the bar are mostly full. Black tables surround the bar, and then beyond that, blue velvet booths for anyone desiring a little more privacy.

Hayden guides me to a U-shaped booth with a killer view of the ocean. I'm distracted watching the waves lap at the shore as I slide in and don't realize I've scooted too far until I'm practically on his lap.

"Oh! I'm sorry." I start to scoot away, but he stops me with a firm hand on my inner thigh.

My heart sinks, and tension tugs between my legs.

That opens up new horror. I've never felt aroused by a man so quickly before.

Then again, I've never let a man put his hand on my inner thigh like this...

Not that I'm letting him. I want to move it. I know I *should* move it. But there's something hard in his gaze, something commanding that conveys wordlessly that I shouldn't.

My stomach pitches, but I ignore the warning. It's only his hand, after all. I'm being silly.

I swallow and reach for the little black menu standing up on the table. My eyes scan it as if I'm deciding on a drink, but I can't concentrate long enough to read any of the words. I can't focus on anything but the weight of his big, warm hand on my inner thigh.

Why isn't he moving it?

Does he think I'll scoot away if he does?

My chest feels tight as I look around to see if anyone else notices, but of course no one does. No one cares if his hand is on my thigh. They're busy enjoying their own dates.

When his hand does finally move, it's not away like I expect. He gives my thigh a gentle squeeze. It feels so intimate, so familiar. The sort of thing a lover would do, not a first date.

I shouldn't have gone out with him.

This was a mistake.

"I think you need a drink," he murmurs, plucking the menu from my nervous fingers and scanning it himself, his hand never leaving my thigh. "Do you have any strong preferences or dislikes when it comes to alcohol?"

I shake my head, unable to find my words.

His eyebrows rise. "Really? No preference whatsoever?"

"I don't enjoy whiskey," I say since it's somehow all I can think of.

He eyes me skeptically, but doesn't press. When the server comes over, he orders bourbon for himself and the house sangria for me.

I didn't expect him to order for me, but I didn't hate it.

His daring hand inches higher, nearing my panties. I'm not sure if it's inadvertent or deliberate. By the time the server brings our drinks, my whole body feels warm, and I'm completely parched. I'm surprised to see a whole pitcher of sangria when he only ordered it for me.

"Can I get a glass of water as well?" I ask.

She nods and says she'll be right back.

"Thirsty?" Hayden asks, his tone lightly amused.

"I like to have two drinks. It's a weird quirk of mine. I always like to have water as an alternative, even if I probably won't drink it."

He watches my face as if he finds that tidbit fascinating. "Afraid you won't like what you initially picked out?" He grabs his bourbon and takes a slow sip. "Are you indecisive, Miss Cane?"

I can't even decide whether to say yes or no, so I guess I am. It's less about fear of making a claim one way or the other. I can't stop thinking about his hand between my thighs. It's so... so inappropriate.

His pinkie inches higher, and my breath hitches. I grab my glass and gulp down more of it than I should have.

"Tell me about your last date," he says.

I place the glass down, looking at it instead of him. "It wasn't very good."

"No?"

I shake my head.

"Why not?"

"We didn't have any chemistry or anything to talk about. He was a doctor who worked all the time. I was a single mom dance instructor. I tried to talk to him about things, but it didn't seem like he had any real interest in my opinions or hobbies. I thought the date was horrible, but when we went to leave, he still tried to make out with me and invite me back to his place. I think he just wanted..."

"To fuck you."

His crude words make my eyes widen. Averting my gaze from his, I murmur, "Yes."

"Is that so awful? Don't you ever go out just for a brief physical connection?"

I shake my head. "Not really my thing. Generally speaking, I don't have sexual feelings toward someone until I've established an emotional connection. I can't want a man I don't already like."

Or I had thought that until tonight.

I'm not sure I like him—*not sure I don't, either*—but I definitely know he isn't someone I should be sexually attracted to. I could never act on a sexual attraction to Landon Atwater's father.

Needing to steer my thoughts away from sexy things

and back into more appropriate waters, I clear my throat and ask, "Did you have a chance to speak with Landon about how he's been treating Parker?"

"Not yet. I will. You're trying to change the subject."

My eyes widen. "What? No, I..."

His hand slides as high as it can without pushing his palm flush against me, his fingertips brushing against my pussy through the material of my panties.

"Hayden." My spine stiffens. I know it has to be deliberate, and he's making me so flushed. It's indecent to touch someone this way in public. Finally, I reach down and grab his hand, tugging it out from under my skirt. "I believe your hand is lost."

He smirks. "I believe it knows right where it wants to go."

"I'm not going to sleep with you."

"Good news. I don't fuck with my hand. I can think of some other things I could do with it, though."

So can I, and my cheeks heat even more. "You're a very bold man."

"And you're a woman who keeps her passion locked up in a prison cell. Perhaps you need a man like me to help you break it out."

I fight the urge to tug my skirt down so it's not riding up so high, but I don't want to draw more attention to the area. "Just because I don't want you groping me while we're in a public place does not mean I keep my passions locked up. And I certainly *don't* need a man like you. I've done just fine by myself all these years."

"I wasn't suggesting we get married," he says, his hand sliding back to my thigh but not being so daring now. He grabs his bourbon and takes a sip. "I would like to peel back those defenses and pound past your barriers, though. I want to see what you look like in a moment of unrestrained passion, to taste your whimpers on my lips. I think you should reconsider your position."

Mercifully, the server brings over my water. I try to take advantage of her presence at the table to scoot away from him, but when I try, he locks his hand around my thigh again.

"Stop," he says casually.

Eyes wide, I turn my head to stare at him. "Get your hand off my thigh."

He glances down at his watch. "Eleven minutes."

"Excuse me?"

He releases my thigh and looks over at me. "You've been uncomfortable from the moment I put my hand on your leg, but it took you eleven minutes to tell me point-blank to move it."

"It'll take me two more to call a cab and go wait for it alone if you keep critiquing my behavior."

Hayden grins. "I like you. I'm not trying to be an asshole. I'm trying to help."

"I don't need your help."

"Actually, you do. Remember when you burst into my office asking for it? You're uncomfortable making other people uncomfortable, so you'll sit in your discomfort to spare them, even if you don't know or particularly like them. Don't do that. If someone isn't considerate of your comfort, don't be considerate of theirs. Next time your neighbor approaches, tell him immediately to go away. Tell him he's not welcome on your property, and if he doesn't leave, you'll call the police. If he ignores your direct warning and puts his hands on you, knee him as hard as you can right between the legs. Then follow through—call the police. There's no guarantee your efforts will be enough to protect you, but I *can* guarantee that inaction will embolden him to take things even further. This neighbor of yours isn't a good guy. Everything else aside, a good guy would never make insinuations about your teenage daughter. You need to make your boundaries with him very clear, and the moment he crosses them, you do something about it."

Just the thought of it makes me nervous. "I've never been great at confrontation."

"We all have different strengths," he says. "I understand this is harder for you, but that's why he's targeting you. He caught on to that, too. He's not the type to pick on someone his own size. He picks on someone smaller so he knows he'll win. He's a wimp. I've never met the man, and he disgusts me, but some people are like that, and they have to be put in their place."

"I think part of the problem is I'm pretty tolerant, so maybe my boundaries aren't the same as everyone else's. My boundary wasn't crossed when he first started being a jerk, but he kept coming until he crossed my boundary, and then it was too late. He was too confident he could walk all over me."

Hayden nods. "He's an asshole. We'll deal with it and get rid of him. Don't worry too much about it. Just giving you some tips."

I nod, tucking my hair behind my ears, but I'm not sure he's right. Yeah, he addressed the issue tonight with Lisa, and I'm sure she will have something to say about it when Brent gets home, but that doesn't mean my problem is solved. Even if Brent is exactly the kind of worm Hayden thinks he is, the threat of Hayden is all that protects me right now.

We're neighbors. Brent will realize pretty quickly that Hayden isn't coming around anymore, and it would only take a sweeping gaze to see that no additional cameras have been installed.

Hayden's bluff may have bought me a reprieve, but where will I be when he disappears from my life again?

Right back where I was when I stormed into his office, but having also provoked Brent by telling his wife.

THE PITCHER of sangria was definitely the right call.

I knew Gemma needed to loosen up. First dates make a lot of people uncomfortable, and she's probably one of them. Most people worry about putting their best foot forward and impressing whomever they're out with.

Me, I've never worried about it. Like me as I am, or fuck off and I'll find someone who does. But Gemma and I are nothing alike, as far as I can tell. Complete and utter opposites in every imaginable way.

I want to know if that difference extends to the bedroom.

As she has consumed more sangria, she has warmed right up. She sways to the music as if she doesn't have a passing thought to give to what anyone else thinks. She smiles easily and often, so I know she's having a good time. As the pitcher empties, she begins to lean on me more, her lowered inhibitions making room for her desires—and the attraction to me she won't stop fighting.

I place my hand on her thigh again, but this time, she doesn't stiffen or tell me to move it. This time, she doesn't want me to.

She leans her head on my shoulder and lets her eyes drift closed. "I'm sleepy."

Absently, I kiss her temple as I slide my hand up her thigh.

She sighs softly.

"Do you want to go?" I ask.

"No," she murmurs, but she probably thinks I mean to end the date.

I don't.

This date is ending only one way—with me inside her. I've already rented us a room, but I didn't tell her earlier because I knew she would panic.

Right now, she's far from panicked. She's relaxed and languid. When my hand slips beneath her skirt, she spreads her legs just a bit to make more room for me.

I feel the breath rush out of her as I drag my fingertips across her pussy. I wish she hadn't worn panties, but I knew she would be. No one has brought Gemma in touch with her naughty side yet. A damned shame, too.

I brush my lips across her temple. "You like that?"

"Mm-hmm," she murmurs, her eyes still closed.

"If we were alone, I'd push you back in this booth and climb between these lovely legs of yours." I press a little harder, pushing the tip of my finger into her even through the panties. "I'd spread you open and devour your pussy until you couldn't control yourself anymore. Bucking, writhing, sinking your fingers into my hair and pulling as I drive you closer and closer to the brink."

"Oh my," she whispers.

It's so fucking cute how surprised she is. It's like no one has ever uttered a few dirty words in her ear before.

What kind of fucking idiots has she been dating?

It's the right moment, so I kiss her temple again and tell her, "I got us a room."

"I can't stay the night with you," she says, but this time it sounds more like a regret than something she's resolved to.

"We don't have to stay the whole night. We don't *have* to do anything. I just figured we could go there to have a little more privacy." I can feel she still isn't convinced, but she wants to go, so I lean closer and tease, "You wouldn't leave me without a good night kiss, would you?"

She sighs, but this time not with pleasure. "You make it so hard to resist you."

"Do I?" I murmur with feigned innocence.

She opens her eyes and shoots me a look. "You know you do."

I smile. "Why don't you finish what's left in your glass, and we'll get out of here?"

With some effort, she lifts herself off me and grabs her sangria. "This is a bad idea," she murmurs as she drains the rest of her glass, then takes a couple of sips of her mostly untouched water.

I have to disagree. This is the best idea I've had in a while.

Once we've finished our drinks and I've paid the bill, Gemma and I follow the path to the hotel lobby. When we get inside, she gasps and looks around, admiring my brother's lavish hotel.

I'm far less impressed and far more interested in showing her the room—and not for the décor.

I reserved a king bed with a view just in case we did end up staying until morning. I seldom bring women home, but Gemma seems like the type of woman who very much expects to spend all night with you after a fuck, and I have no problem spending the night with her.

My only concern is her daughter.

Landon knows not to worry if I don't come home when I go out, but I'm not sure her daughter does. I grabbed Gemma's phone number when I was doing my homework prior to the date, but I didn't think to look up her daughter's, and I don't know Gemma's phone code, so I won't be able to open it once she falls asleep.

If I tell her beforehand to text her daughter, I run the risk of her getting cold feet and leaving. She's all but admitted to being a bit wary of making decisions, so maybe it's best to take it out of her hands and make the call for her.

We'll both have a good time. She just needs to get out of her own way.

The room is dark when I scan the key and open the door. We have an ocean view with a little balcony where we can have breakfast in the morning if she stays. I bet she'll like that.

Gemma's holding my hand again. I can't remember the last time I held hands with a woman, but she has held my hand several times tonight, and I kind of like it. It's a trusting gesture of affection.

The thought whispers across my mind that I might be taking advantage of that trust right now. She made it pretty clear she didn't want to sleep with me tonight, but I think I can change her mind. I don't even think I *need* to change her mind. I know she's attracted to me, even wants me, she just thinks she has her reasons not to do it.

I disagree. I don't care about some tiff between our kids. That's a ridiculous reason not to explore our obvious attraction to one another.

As soon as the door closes behind us, I let her get ahead of me. She dangles her purse and walks a bit unsteadily into the room, admiring the simple décor.

"I would've gone for a bigger room for an extended stay, but I figured we only really needed a bed tonight."

She giggles and turns around to look at me with that lazy smile on her lovely face. "That sounds so naughty."

I come up behind her, encircling her waist and taking her purse so I can set it aside on the wet bar. "Would you like a drink?"

"I think I've had more than enough to drink," she assures me, leaning back into my embrace.

I pull her hair aside so I can bend to kiss her neck. As I do, I peel off her sparkly blazer and toss it aside, too.

"You're undressing me," she murmurs.

"Very astute." I kiss her earlobe, and she shivers.

Leaning back a bit, I kiss the ball of her shoulder, then work loose the button on the back of her blouse.

"You shouldn't take off my top."

"Why not?" I ask easily. "I've seen more than this already when you stormed into my office."

She laughs at herself. "In my stupid belly dancing clothes."

I smirk. "They weren't stupid at all." I tug the blouse down off her arms, then push it past her slim hips. I kneel to pull it the rest of the way, then unzip her skirt and pull that down, too.

"Wait a minute," she murmurs, realizing she's down to her bra and panties.

Rather than wait, I lean in and kiss her hip bone. She sucks in a breath. I kiss my way along her toned lower abdomen and don't stop when I get to her panties.

Her sighs become bigger and heavier as I kiss my way from the top of her pantyline lower until I'm kissing her pussy through the fabric. I kiss the insides of her thighs, then return to her pussy, covering her with my mouth.

"Oh, Hayden," she murmurs tremulously, her fingers sliding through my hair.

"Get on the bed," I tell her, freeing my hair from her hands and rising.

She walks backward but hesitates before getting on the mattress, so I give her a little shove.

She's too drunk for good reflexes, so she falls back against the soft bed with a little giggle.

I'm wearing too many layers of clothing, so I start strip

ping them off. Once I'm down to my boxer briefs, I join her on the bed, climbing on top of her and looking down at her.

Her big brown eyes are so open, so fond, I can't resist kissing her.

I scarcely taste her lips at first, just a quick brush. Her lips are so soft beneath mine, and I want more, so I crush her with my weight, catching her moan in my mouth and tangling my fingers in her soft hair. Her instinct is still to shut me out, but I force my way past her lips and she gives immediately, making room for me and kissing me back as her hands come to rest on my back.

I want her tits free, so while I'm kissing her senseless, I shift her body beneath mine and reach back to unclasp her bra. The material gives, and I peel it away, tossing it on the floor behind us.

I don't stop kissing her, so she doesn't have a chance to object. My palm covers the soft globe and she exhales sharply, but I catch it on my lips and make her go right back to kissing me without giving her a chance to breathe.

I love the way she follows my lead even though some part of her knows I'm taking her somewhere she swore she wouldn't go.

That reality seems to pierce the fog of lust, and she tries to pull back, but I have her trapped beneath my weight. Between kisses, she murmurs, "Hayden," but I tug her head back by the hair and slant my mouth over hers more aggressively.

She resists a little, but she doesn't fight. Her body

wants the same thing I want. It's her mind that isn't entirely on board.

My cock hardens to steel as she moves her little dancer's body beneath me. Her hands come up and push against my chest as mine skims her side before I grab her other tit.

Some part of me recognizes that I'm not giving her a chance to object. I know she's slow to ask, that in all likelihood she'll let me go further than she's comfortable going before she finally tells me she wants me to stop, but fuck, I don't want her to do that.

I push her thighs farther apart and butt my cock against her pussy, wishing I had stripped off her panties before I got on top of her. I wasn't prepared for how quickly lust would drag me under. I can't remember the last time I wanted a woman with this intensity—to be willing to bend her will and shake the world beneath her feet if it means what I want will fall into my hands as a result.

Actually, I can, and the last time I wanted something that much, I couldn't have it.

I would have traded away all the rest of my days for one more night with Sally, but once she was gone, no amount of bargaining with the gods could get me what I wanted. Not ever again.

The memory fuels my need to hold tight to Gemma at this moment. It's been so long since I've wanted something like this, but she's not one more night with my dead wife. I *can* have her—and I will.

I break away from Gemma's lips to kiss her collarbone —short, greedy little kisses. I move lower and kiss her breasts, then lower still. I move down her stomach, leaving kisses along the way. Then, finally, I hook my fingers in the waistband of her black panties and pull them down.

"Wait," she says, reaching for them to keep her safety barrier in place.

"I want to taste you," I tell her, pushing her hand away and dragging her panties off.

I toss the panties and bend down, fighting the instinct to latch onto her pussy right away. She's too skittish, so I have to ease her in.

I kiss her inner thigh like I did when she was standing, but this time, I bite them, too. She gasps and shudders as I'm gentle, then rough, and when I can't take it anymore, I push my tongue into her, groaning at the taste of her arousal on my tongue.

She cries out as my tongue brushes her sensitive clit. I could take my time tasting her, but my aching cock wants to get inside her. I don't waste time exploring. I zero right in on her clit and fuck that sensitive little nub with my tongue until her thighs are trembling and broken cries emanate from her lovely throat.

Her nails dig into the bedding. She pants and bucks and begs. "Hayden."

Fuck, that's hot.

I eat her with abandon, her desperate cries sinking hooks into me and making me crave her even more.

When she comes, she cries out and tries to twist away

from me, but I don't fucking think so. I let go of her long enough for her to roll over on her tummy, but only so I can shuck the last of my clothing and roll a condom on my dick.

I come up behind her, forcing her thighs apart and making room for myself between them. She's still tummy down on the bed, but I don't ask her to get up on her knees because there's a chance she'll say no.

I don't typically fuck in this position. It feels predatory, like something I'm doing *to* her before she can stop me instead of something I'm doing *with* her. Without warning, I push my cock into her sensitive pussy and drive deep.

She cries out as I fill her, bracing her hands against the mattress. She's fucking tight even though she just came, and it takes some effort to bury myself all the way to the hilt.

"Hayden."

Fuck, she feels so good.

I'm terrified she's going to stop me. So terrified I cover her mouth as I push into her again. I can't even think straight, she feels so fucking good. I hear little muffled cries against my palm as I fuck her, but I'm too consumed with the heaven of her body to pay them much heed.

I can't kiss her the way I want to since she's facedown on the bed, but with my hand over her mouth, it's easy to pull her back like a bow and kiss the side of her face before lowering her and driving into her again.

I'm so lost to the pleasure of possessing her that I can't

be entirely sure she's enjoying herself as much as I am until her cries against my palm grow more desperate and broken, and I feel her pussy choking the life out of my cock.

Fuck.

She's coming, and it throws me over the edge. I shove deep and join her, cursing and groaning as I thrust through the intensity of my own orgasm.

The high lasts longer than it usually does, but when it finally stops, I let go of her mouth and collapse against her on the bed. I press my lips to her bare shoulder blade. I want to kiss her everywhere, but I'm too fucking spent to move.

Gemma lies beneath me quietly, pinned beneath my weight, trapped tummy down on the mattress. Awareness that I'm probably crushing her washes over me, so I move off her body with some effort.

I don't want to let her go, but when I reach out to pull her into my arms, she moves away and sits up.

I'm blissed out and inordinately pleased, but she looks sober as she scoots toward the edge of the bed.

I figure she may want to go to the bathroom to clean up, so I don't think much of it until she starts gathering up her clothes.

What is she doing?

I don't want her to get dressed already. I want to hold her for a while, maybe explore her naked body more thoroughly once I've fully recovered. I've never felt like I needed to take a woman in stages before, but it still feels like I'm barely acquainted with her body, and I want to know every inch.

"Come back to bed," I tell her.

She shakes her head, bending down and stepping into her panties. "It's late. I need to get home."

I don't like that.

Don't like the tone of her voice, either.

Sitting up, I look her over, and the doubt that clouded my thoughts before my cock took over resurfaces. "Are you all right?"

"Yes, I'm fine," she says quietly, pulling on her skirt and zipping it up.

"Are you sure?"

If she's not, I'll fix it. The problem is, I'm not sure she'll tell me.

"That wasn't supposed to happen," she says, pushing her arms through the holes and clasping her bra behind her back. "I told you I didn't want to..." She trails off, shaking her head as if she doesn't want to think about it anymore, then she grabs her blouse and pulls it over her head. "It doesn't matter."

I frown, watching as she pulls on her blazer and grabs her purse. "Gemma, don't leave."

She pulls her hair out of the back of the blazer and turns toward the door.

I get off the bed because I'm not about to let her walk out that door until we've resolved this.

"I have to get home. Parker will wonder why—"

I catch her around the waist, turning her around and

putting my body in front of her so I can force her backward toward the bed.

She avoids my gaze and retreats on instinct.

I may have been giving her tips on curbing those prey-like instincts with her shitty neighbor, but to be honest, I don't want her to learn to fight them with me. I *like* her instincts. I enjoy the way she retreats and makes me chase her. I'm not used to it at all, but it's intriguing.

A part of me is even drawn to the vulnerable look in her big brown eyes as she gazes up at me once I have her cornered—when I'm bending her to my will—and she looks like she damn well knows it.

It's like there's something in her DNA that stirs the predatory instincts of those around her while at the same time instilling in them a desire to protect her.

Whatever instinct she triggers, it screams: she's *mine* to play with, no one else's.

No one has ever awoken this side of me before. I'm an asshole when I need to be, sure, but I wasn't bullshitting her when I told her I've never been attracted to easy targets. It's mean to refer to her that way, and I don't mean any insult at all, but there's just something about her. Maybe it's her big doe eyes that trigger the primal hunter buried deep inside me.

She softens when confronted with a predator, too. Makes the dance and the act of capturing her even more satisfying.

I think she's right about her boundaries. From what she told me, she was probably giving her neighbor the energy she's giving me right now when he cornered her, and I can definitely see why he liked it. I bet his wife would never let him get away with stalking her and cornering her. Most women wouldn't. But then he stepped over Gemma's generous boundary and mentioned her daughter, so she snapped out of it and told him to fuck off.

Gemma's boundaries not being where everyone else's are makes her very interesting to me. Ordinary people are all more or less the same with no surprises. But with Gemma, it's like being handed a map I've never seen before. I want to explore every inch—see where I'm allowed to go and where I'm not.

I'm fairly certain I just made her have sex with me, but when I pull her close and move her arm around my waist to make sure she'll let me hold her, she does. She even holds me back.

If her boundaries are this generous, there's little chance I'll ever step over them. I take what I want, but I'm not a fucking pervert. I would never threaten harm to her or her loved ones.

But I'm damn sure not going to be resisted.

I know she wants the same thing, she's just afraid to take it for herself, so I'll have to step in and see that she gets what she needs.

I lean down to brush my lips against hers. She's so fucking soft. I sink my fingers into her hair and cradle her head as I kiss her.

She tastes fucking incredible.

I need more of her, so much more.

I thought one night might be enough to cure me of my interest in the intriguing little belly dancer, but I was very wrong. I've tasted her *and* fucked her, and I feel like I haven't even had a sample. If anything, my appetite for her now feels more enormous than it was before I had her.

Seeming to catch on that she's not leaving unless I let her, she kisses me back. Her tone is more cajoling and less reserved when she says, "I really have to go home."

She's telling me, but asking at the same time.

She needs me to let her go for the moment, but it doesn't mean she won't come back.

It doesn't feel so final this time.

Of course, she could just be playing nice to get out of my snare with no intent of ever returning, but that's not going to work for me.

Caressing her jaw, I smile faintly and ask, "You know what I thought the first time I saw you?"

"Who is this lunatic, and where are her clothes?"

I smirk. "No."

She smiles, seeming more open again. "What did you think?"

"I thought you were there to grant me a wish."

"A wish?" she questions, laughing.

I nod. "But you know what? I'm going to grant yours instead." It's not selfless, really. Now that I've stalked and pounced on her myself, I don't want her sleazy neighbor coming anywhere near my territory. "I'll solve your Hartley problem. You don't have to file a restraining order or worry about a bill. I don't want you to do anything else. I'll handle it from here."

"Was this my payment?" she asks in a tone intended to be light, but I can tell it expresses real concern as she avoids my gaze.

I tip her chin up, not letting her get away with the avoidance. "No," I say clearly. "This was a date, and I want another one soon."

Carefully extracting herself from my embrace, she says, "I already told you this can't go anywhere."

"I don't agree." Her mouth opens, but I hold up a hand to stop her. "I'll handle my son."

She isn't willing to agree, but she doesn't want to argue with me about it either, so she plays her avoidance game and tells me she needs to get going.

I'll let her go for the moment, but I make her wait while I get ready so I can take her home myself.

When we pull into her driveway, I start to open my car door to walk her inside, but she asks me not to.

I know she doesn't want to make noise and wake her daughter, but I suspect she also doesn't want her daughter to know she was out with me.

I relent, allowing her to escape my company, but not before I tell her, "I'll see you again soon."

She smiles but doesn't agree. "Thank you for a nice night, Hayden."

Then she closes the car door, walks to her front door, and disappears inside the house without so much as a backward glance.

MY ALARM CLOCK GOES OFF, alerting me that I need to get up and prepare for my day.

Instead, I turn it off and roll over, wrapping my arms around my pillow and hugging it snugly against me. I roll onto it a little more so I'm on my tummy, and memories of last night resurface.

Hayden's rough hands parting my thighs.

His thick cock shoving into me.

When he pushed all the way in, I felt fuller than I ever had before. I didn't get a chance to *see* his cock, but I knew it had to be huge when I felt all of him shoved inside me.

And then the way he grabbed me and covered my mouth with his hand, invading my body whether I wanted him to or not.

His skin smelled so good.

He smelled manly and capable as he drove me closer and closer to a second orgasm.

A *second* orgasm.

With the men who came before him, I was pretty lucky if I got one.

Our encounter definitely wasn't how I imagined it when he touched me in the booth at the bar, but it was surprisingly hot. It felt primal, like a claiming. I've never had a man handle me that way, and I felt possessed in a way I'd never experienced before.

I don't know how I feel about having an experience like that with someone I barely know, though. Someone I have no plans to see again.

I guess now I can officially say I've had a one-night stand.

The doorbell rings, finally forcing me out of bed. I grab a robe and slip it on, then I grab my phone off its charger and hurry downstairs.

When I open the door, a man is standing there in denim jeans and a T-shirt with a yellow ball cap on his head.

"How are you doing today?" he asks politely.

"Good." I pull my robe tighter and offer a tiny smile. "Can I help you with something?"

He holds up a clipboard and offers me a pen. "I just need you to open your garage door and sign this work order so we can go ahead and get started."

I frown. "Work order? I'm afraid you're at the wrong house. I don't have any work to be done."

The man frowns and looks down at the clipboard. "Says here Hayden Atwater requested service. Is that your husband?"

The surprise melts out of me, and I shake my head. "No, it isn't, but I know who that is. What exactly did he say I was having done?"

"Security camera installation. It's already paid for. Won't take long, we'll be out of your hair in no time."

I shake my head. "Can you excuse me for just one moment? I need to call Mr. Atwater."

The man is confused, but not knowing what else to do, he nods his head and turns back to talk to his crew.

Sighing, I call Hayden's office and tell his secretary I need to speak with him about an urgent matter. A moment later, Hayden picks up the phone.

"What are you doing?" I demand without so much as a hello.

"Good morning to you, too," he answers.

"Good morning," I mutter, unable to ignore my manners entirely. "Now, would you care to explain what you think you're doing?"

"I think I'm working. Boring stuff, really. Not worth talking about. What about you? How's your day so far?"

"There are men in my driveway wanting to install security cameras they say *you* ordered."

"Correct. It occurred to me that with the neighbor issues you've been having, cameras would be a good idea for real, so I ordered some to be installed right away."

"You can't just order cameras to be installed in my home without my permission, Hayden. This is *my* house, not yours."

"So I should have the one in your bedroom taken out?"

My jaw falls open. "*What?*"

He laughs. "I'm kidding. When would I have had a camera installed? Besides, only a crazy person would do that and then tell you about it." I hear a noise, like he's covering the phone to say hello to someone else—probably the client he's meeting with. Then he comes back to the phone. "I have to go now, but everything should be taken care of. I'm paying for the cameras and the installation. All you have to do is sign the paper because it is your property."

"That's..." I sigh. "Actually, that's really nice of you, but also very inappropriate."

"I'm going to make you an 'inappropriate jar.' You know how most people have swear jars? Every time you say that word, you have to drop a quarter in. We'll be paying for vacations in no time. If you need anything else, just text me, all right? Easier to sneak in a response between tasks."

"I don't have your cell phone number."

"I'll text you."

Does he have *my* cell phone number?

I hate that he's rushing me off the phone because I have more questions about this camera installation business. He really should have asked if it was something I even wanted, but he should have *at least* told me before springing an installation appointment on me.

I go back outside to ask the installation guy how all this works and sign his paper.

By the time I get back inside, Parker is downstairs, frowning as she peeks out the window.

"What's going on out there?"

Crap. I don't know whether to pile more little white lies on top of the existing ones, or if I should just tell her.

Then again, this whole Hayden thing is only temporary. As soon as he solves my neighbor problem, he'll be out of our lives for good.

I don't want to upset her for no reason, and she'll never know if I don't tell her. The only *possible* way for her to find out would be if Landon said something to her about it, but in order for that to happen, Hayden would have to mention it to him.

That seems unlikely. From what I've seen so far, I don't think they share as much as Parker and I do.

"I'm having a few cameras installed," I tell her casually, bending the truth to its breaking point.

Her frown deepens. "Why?"

"Just for extra security. I'm tired of the juvenile pranks eating up so much of my time, and this should put a stop to them. Next time someone does anything to our property, there will be video evidence, so I'll be able to take immediate action."

"That's a good idea," Parker says with a nod, walking around the island to grab a cereal bowl out of the cupboard. "We should have thought of that sooner."

I did. I just couldn't afford good cameras and professional installation, and I didn't trust myself to install the cheap ones.

While Parker fixes herself a bowl of cereal, I grab some fresh pineapple out of the refrigerator.

My phone vibrates on the table. I glance over at it, but do a double take when I see a phone number I don't have saved and a text that says, "What color genie outfit are you wearing today?"

I grab the phone quickly, but tell myself not to act suspicious. Parker isn't paying attention, anyway; she's texting on her phone.

I probably shouldn't answer. There's no reason to engage with him beyond what's necessary.

I do, anyway.

"Blue," I answer.

"My favorite color," he replies back. "You should send me a picture."

Obviously, I don't do that, but I do save his phone number in case I need to contact him again about his intrusion in my life, or even my annoying neighbor.

It's recital night—one of them, anyway. Technically, there are recitals tonight and tomorrow, but tonight's show runs longer, and it's the one with all my classes.

Parker comes to help me keep my outfits straight. Mothers help their kids change, but I still need to change my own costumes as quickly as possible so I can get to the students and parents and help resolve any problems they might have.

"Are you sure you don't want to watch from the audience?" I ask Parker as she moves around me, smoothing down the gold sequins and looking over my tap dancing outfit.

"No, I'm fine watching on the sidelines," she assures me, checking my black tights for runs. "Perfect," she says, pulling out her cell phone. "Now, let me get a picture before you go dance and mess up all my hard work."

I grin at her and strike a pose.

This outfit is one of my favorites: a top hat, a gold sequined tuxedo top with a bow tie, and black short shorts with black tights underneath. I have a cane, and so do all of the adorable little kids in my 7-9 tap class.

I gather up my kids once Parker gets her picture, then we all head out on stage and take our places.

The night goes smoothly, all things considered. One of my creative movement kids gets turned around, and another picks her nose on stage. The audience laughs, of course, because she's five.

The night goes by in a blur of counting little heads and quick costume changes. Finally, toward the end of the night, I get to perform with my older 12-14 kids, and then my belly dancing class is the last of my classes. There's one teacher after me with a group of high school seniors doing ballet, but I'm completely beat by the time they dance.

The show closes, and all the dancers and instructors head backstage.

Thankfully, my amazing daughter has already packed up all my discarded costumes. I don't bother changing out of the belly dancing one since we're heading straight home, and now that the show is over I have to visit my students to tell them how great they were.

I get a carnation wrapped in tinfoil from a blond-haired little boy, the only boy in my creative movement class.

"Aw, that's so sweet of you, Jamie. Thank you," I say, giving him a hug. "You did such a great job tonight. You were even better than me!"

He's shy, but he blushes and smiles, then returns to his mom's side. She thanks me for all my work with him over the summer, and then they leave.

Slowly, every last student trickles out, so I head back to my dressing room, where Parker waits with the suitcase full of my costumes.

"Do you know who the best daughter in town is?"

"Just in town?" she jokes. "I did all this without pay."

"Fine, your greatness extends beyond our locality. You are officially the best daughter in the world. Maybe the *universe*."

She cracks a smile and wheels the luggage toward the door. "I have your makeup bag. Make sure I didn't forget anything. I'll take this stuff out to the car."

"I owe you an abundance of Twizzlers," I call as she heads out the door.

"And I'm picking all the movies we watch tonight," she calls back.

I smile, turning around to double-check that I'm not

leaving anything behind. Once I'm satisfied that I'm not, I turn off the lights so I can leave.

The lobby is still bustling with dancers talking to their guests, most with an armful of flowers. I'm so distracted watching them as I make my way toward the exit doors that I walk right into someone.

"Oh, I'm so sorry," I say, backing up as my gaze snaps to the person I ran into.

My tummy tumbles when I look up into the handsome face of Hayden Atwater. I take in his sultry smile and the glint of mischief in his eyes, the handsome blue suit stretched over his impressive physique. In his arms rests a gorgeous bouquet of blue and purple orchids.

He holds them out to me.

Flowers for me?

"What are you doing here?" I ask cautiously, not reaching for the bouquet.

"You never sent me that picture, so I had to come see your blue costume for myself." He smirks, nodding at the single white carnation in my hand. "I figured every dancer deserves flowers after their performance, but I see someone beat me to it."

I nod, bringing the carnation to my nose and inhaling the lovely scent. "Yep. He was rather dashing, too."

"Clearly a believer in the 'less is more' mentality. I especially like the tinfoil vase."

"He's very adept at arts and crafts." I look over the beautiful bouquet he brought me. "Yours are lovely, too. Even without the foil."

"Well, if they can impress without tinfoil, I must have made the right choice."

I smile, taking the bouquet in my left arm and lifting them so I can smell them. "I love orchids." I bring my gaze back to his. "Thank you. That was very thoughtful. Did you just come to do a costume check and deliver flowers, or did you watch the performance?"

He draws a ticket out of his breast pocket. "Paid my fifteen dollars and everything. I very much enjoyed all of your costumes. Who do I have to contact about arranging a private show?"

I shake my head and look down at my flowers, memories of last night creeping up on me. "No private shows for you. You shouldn't even be here. I don't know what this has to do with handling my neighbor problem."

"Well, obviously, if Brent sees you coming home without flowers, he'll make certain assumptions about the kind of boyfriend I am."

I smile because he's so full of shit. "Of course. Wouldn't want Brent to form a bad opinion of your boyfriend abilities."

He nods, his gaze moving slowly over my body before returning to my face. More seriously, he says, "You danced your ass off tonight. You must be hungry. Let me take you out to dinner."

"I am hungry, but I can't go to dinner with you. My daughter's waiting in the car."

"She can't drive herself home?"

"She's also hungry," I state.

"Then bring her, too."

That surprises me so much, the smile falls off my face. There have been a lot of times dating as a single mom when I *wished* a man would say something like that.

Some part of me even thinks Parker might like Hayden, but since she doesn't know he's the one I was out with last night, I can't just spring something like that on her. She might not be comfortable saying no, but also not be comfortable hanging out with her mortal enemy's father.

I don't want to put her in an awkward position, and I'm not prepared to clue her in that I've spent time with him outside of his office, anyway.

"I don't think that's a good idea."

"Why not?"

I shoot him a look. "You know why not."

"I won't invite Landon."

"And how do you think he'll respond if he finds out you took us to dinner without him? Honestly, Hayden. He makes her life hard enough."

"I told you, I'll talk to him about that. There's no reason to think he would find out about my taking you two out to dinner. It could be beneficial to hear her side of the story. It will give me a better idea of what I need to bring up when I do talk to him about it."

I shake my head, but I'm more tempted by the idea than he can imagine.

Too tempted.

"We aren't dating," I state, partially to remind him but

mostly to remind myself. It would be easy to get confused with the sex and the flowers, his pushy insistence on taking care of me and my problems when he doesn't have to. "I don't introduce my daughter to men I'm not dating. I hardly introduce her to men I *am* dating. Her stability is the highest priority for me, and I don't see the point in sharing information that might upset her when this isn't going anywhere."

My reasonable statement seems to irritate him. "There you go saying that again."

"It's true. We both know it's true. Now, thank you for the flowers. They're lovely. I'm glad you enjoyed the show, and I appreciate the cameras, but I really have to go."

I try to brush past him, but Hayden grabs my arm, halting my departure.

I look up at him, wordlessly requesting release.

He looks back, wordlessly denying it. "Tomorrow, then."

His hard tone brooks no arguments, but I give him one, anyway.

"No."

His eyes narrow. "I told you I want to see you again."

I tug at my arm, but he doesn't let go. "And I told you I'm not interested in dating."

"We aren't dating. We're just spending time together. Preferably without clothes on, but I'm flexible."

"Hayden..." I tug my arm again.

His grip tightens. "I'm not releasing you until you agree to see me again."

"We are in public," I remind him.

"I don't care."

He may not, but I do.

I cast a subtle glance at the people around us, hoping no one notices this brute holding my arm prisoner until I relent and give him his way.

The biggest problem is, a part of me *wants* to relent.

His hand locked around my arm reminds me of last night, the way his hands felt on my body. I can't even remember how long it's been since a man touched me, and never one like this.

Maybe one more "date" wouldn't be the end of the world.

"If I meet you tomorrow, we need to agree it's the last time."

"If you agree to meet me tomorrow, I'll release your arm and let you leave. That's all the ground I'm willing to cede at the moment."

"Why?"

His eyes seem to darken. "Because I'm not finished with you yet."

The truth is simple but hard to hear at the same time. I swallow, my stomach knotting up at the ominous way it sounds.

I won't say I'm not finished with *him* because I would've been done with him already if I had my way.

I'm not entirely averse to the idea of him fucking me again, though. Especially when he holds my arm like this and gazes at me with that hungry look in his eyes.

"One more night. That's all I'll agree to."

His grip on my arm loosens, and I tug it free.

He didn't grip my arm hard enough to hurt me, but I still rub it, feeling the absence of his touch immediately.

"Tomorrow," he says immovably. "I'm off, and so are you."

I don't know how he knows that. I didn't tell him. "Fine. What time?"

"I'll pick you up at two o'clock."

My eyes widen in surprise. "That's early."

"If you want me to be sick of you by the end of the night, we'll have to start early. It's the only way there's even a chance."

I can't help smiling. "I'm not that interesting, I promise."

"You are to me."

His words are so raw, so honest, they rip the breath from my lungs. I feel unsteady on my feet, having him brazenly say a thing like that to me.

I think it's because I know he's not dropping some bullshit line like most guys would be. He truly means it.

A lump forms in my throat, but I try to swallow it down.

I think I could like him, but he's the last man in the world I'm allowed to like.

"I'll see you tomorrow, then," I say softly.

He nods his head once, his gaze never leaving mine. "I look forward to it."

His sincerity tugs on my heartstrings. It's the thing I've desired most but never been able to find in a man.

It's just my luck that it's the first time I stumble across a man who might be everything I've always been looking for, and he might as well be locked up tight in Pandora's box.

WHEN I PULL into Gemma's driveway this afternoon, the garage door is open, and Parker is out of the house as I instructed when I texted her this morning.

I'm not opposed to meeting her daughter, but Gemma clearly is, and the first part of our date has to take place at her house. It's strategic.

Where possible, I like to kill as many birds with a single stone as I can, and I need to feed Gemma *and* let her neighbors know I'm around and not one to fuck with, so I swung by my brother's house first.

"Come on, boy." I leave my things in the car and call Hades out of my back seat.

I must fucking like her to let this massive dog shed all over my fucking car. It's an atrocity.

Hades leaps out gracefully, standing proud and looking around at his new surroundings.

I hear the inner garage door open, and Gemma steps out of the house wearing a white tank top with blue-and-white-striped shorts. They look nautical and hot as hell on her pretty little ass. Just the sight of her smile makes me forget all about any damage the damn dog might have done to my nice leather interior.

Her bright smile drops, her expression growing alarmed as she sees the beast I brought with me. "Um... what is that?"

I smile faintly. "That's a dog. His name is Hades."

"Perfect name. He certainly looks like the devil's dog." Her wary gaze returns to me. "Why is your scary dog at my house?"

"Not my dog. Don't have time for one. I borrowed one of my brother's dogs. He has three—Zeus, Hades, and Hera. They're the ones on the sign at his bar. This one looks the scariest, so he's the one I brought."

Wide-eyed, she says, "This dog looks like a bear and a monster had a baby and he's the result."

That's a very apt description for Hades. He's a black pit bull with blue eyes so light, they're nearly colorless.

"He's very well-trained," I assure her since I can see he makes her uncomfortable. "You don't have to be afraid of him. In fact, it's better if you're not. He can smell fear, and it makes him wary."

Her gaze flits to mine. "Is there a reason you brought your brother's scary-looking, fear-smelling dog to my house?"

"There is." I glance toward her neighbor's house, but no one is outside at the moment. "If your neighbors see this big boy hanging out in your yard, do you think they'll sneak into it to smear cheese on the side of your house?"

She glances at Hades. He looks back at her with an intelligent, intense gaze. "No, I do not," she says, seeing my point. "Is he friendly?"

I nod. "You can pet him. Let him sniff your hand first."

She walks over slowly, then smiles and extends her hand toward him. "Hello, Hades. I'm Gemma."

He sniffs her hand, then licks it to let her know they're good.

I feel the tension start to melt out of her, and he probably does, too.

"You must be thirsty," she says, lightly petting his back. "I'll go get him a bowl of water."

While she runs back inside to get Hades a drink, I grab the blanket and insulated tote I brought with me. I walk Hades over to the yard and command him to lie down and stay put. He watches curiously as I unfold the blanket on the lawn, then start to unpack the cured meats, fruit, and different cheeses.

Gemma comes back out with a mixing bowl full of water for Hades. She puts it down beside him, then grins over at me. "A picnic? I love picnics."

"I am not surprised to hear this," I say, grabbing the chilled champagne out of the side that's packed with ice.

Gemma grins as she sits down on the side of the blanket nearest Hades. I packed extra cheese since I knew we would have him. I grab a cube and hand it to Gemma. "It's his favorite treat. Let's get you some brownie points."

She puts the cheese cube down by his paw. He eyes it, then leans down and eats it.

"He's a big boy," she says. "He'll probably need more than one cube."

"He'll get more in a bit." I grab a plate for myself and pass one to her. "I wasn't sure what you liked, so I brought a bit of everything."

"I see that." She eyes the spread. "I love all of it. Except the olives. Olives are gross."

"There's a restaurant in Paris that might change your mind," I tell her, scooping up a few olives for myself. "They bring out olives to snack on with your drink before the meal, and I don't know what they do to those olives, but they're incredible."

"You've been to Paris?" she asks, wide-eyed.

I nod, knowing the answer before I ask, but I ask anyway. "Have you?"

She shakes her head, smiling. "No. I might be willing to try olives in Paris, but I don't think I'll ever get the chance to go there."

"Would you like to?"

"Oh, yes. Very much."

"Who knows? One day, you might get your chance," I say, the words out before I can think them through. I shouldn't say things like that and make her think I mean with me.

Don't I, though?

Of course not. That's absurd. I haven't traveled with a woman romantically since Sally died.

Gemma looks at me, then drops her gaze to her plate. "Maybe," she says, but she doesn't sound convinced.

I pop open the champagne, startling Hades. Gemma instinctively reaches over and puts a calming hand on his back. He looks over at her, then rests his head back on his paws and lets her pet him.

Gemma thanks me as I pass her a glass. I take a sip from mine, then ask, "So, you've never been married?"

I already know she hasn't. I did a background check on her. But there are certain things you admit, and certain things you don't. It's better for her to think I've gleaned most of the information I have on her because she's shared it with me, not because I have a tendency to disregard privacy and be rather invasive.

She shakes her head. "Parker's father and I were engaged, but we couldn't afford a wedding. Thankfully," she says, rolling her eyes. "Marrying him would have been a terrible decision, but I was a teenager, and I didn't know anything."

My lips tug up. "Who does when they're a teenager?"

"Right?" She grabs a grape, but before popping it into her mouth, she asks, "When did you and your wife get married?"

"As soon as we graduated from college. I actually met her in high school. We started dating senior year and decided to go to the same college so we wouldn't have to be apart. Then she got pregnant with Landon during junior year. Panicked a little because he was definitely not planned, but I told her we would figure it out. I ended up proposing, not a terribly romantic proposal, but more to assure her I was committed and I wouldn't leave her high and dry to chase my own dreams. After we graduated college, but before I started law school, we got married under a waterfall in Costa Rica. The proposal may not have been romantic, but the wedding was. Landon was there, but it was very intimate, just the three of us."

My throat tightens as I think about that day. I find myself staring off into space, lost for a moment in a memory of Sally splashing Landon with water, his dimpled grin as he caught a few droplets in his chubby hand and hurled them back at her. He adored his mother as much as I did. She was the sun in both our lives, and then one day, she was just gone, leaving us both drenched in darkness.

I feel Gemma's hand on mine, and I look over to see her worried eyes peering back at me. "Are you okay?" she asks softly.

I nod, pulling my hand away.

It's a stupid instinct, one I regret immediately, but talking about the family I once had isn't something I ever do with women. I wouldn't even know how.

"Anyway, enough about me." I take a sip of champagne to get myself back on track. "We were talking about you."

"What else do you want to know?" she asks.

"Your last serious relationship. Why didn't it work out?"

She picks up a strawberry, focusing her attention on it

instead of me. "Good question. It wasn't for lack of trying. I made a Herculean effort to hold things together, long past the point when I should have given up." She meets my gaze. "My last serious relationship was Parker's father. I've had boyfriends since, but none of them were deep, committed long-term relationships." She wraps her lips around the strawberry and takes a bite.

My cock stirs with interest, but I try to ignore it. "You haven't had another serious relationship since that one? Really?"

She shakes her head, chewing her strawberry and absently plucking a piece of cheese off her plate. "I haven't met anyone I wanted to commit to. Once I commit, it takes a lot to sever that connection, so I'm pretty choosy. I'm not one of these people who happily bounces from relationship to relationship. When I pick my person, that's my person, and I don't want it to ever change."

I can relate to that. I don't date anymore, but when I did commit, it was forever.

"He cheated on me, and I *still* tried to make it work, but we couldn't get the trust back. I tried to hold things together without it, but that was impossible. I stuck it out for a while anyway just because he was Parker's father and I wanted to keep my family together. I didn't want to alternate holidays and spend every other weekend without her. That sounded awful to me, and he was really irresponsible, so I wasn't sure how he would be with her. Turned out, I didn't have to worry about it. As soon as I dumped him for good, he moved in with some girl. He took Parker for a few hours one day a week for exactly three weeks, then he lost all interest. He visited her from time to time and took us out to dinner once in a while, but since we broke up, she's never even spent the night with him."

I frown. "You don't share custody?"

She shakes her head, leaning back and stretching out her legs. "Nope. It's been years since we've seen him. I don't even know where he lives anymore. Don't care, either."

"Does he at least pay child support?"

She laughs. "No."

I shake my head, unimpressed. "That's his responsibility. You should make him pay."

"I know, but it wasn't worth the fight to me. Honestly, I was just happy not to have to share Parker. I can be a better father to her than he can, anyway. Maybe I'd feel differently if she did, but..." She shrugs. "Parker's a smart kid, and she knows her worth. If he's too big of an idiot to want a relationship with her, she doesn't want one with him, either."

My eyebrows rise, and I nod, impressed. "Takes a lot of maturity to be able to feel that way at such a young age."

She nods proudly. "Like I said, she's super smart. Mature for her age, too. Part of it is probably that I was so young when I had her, and her dad wasn't much support to begin with. It's always been just the two of us, so I guess in some ways she has had to be a little more grown-up than most kids her age. Especially the kids in this town."

The way she says it, she doesn't seem to think much of

the spoiled, entitled brats who live in Baymont. Can't say I blame her, though. "Yeah, I didn't have money growing up, either. Life is a lot different for my son than it was for me."

The mention of my son dims her happiness. I don't want to remind her of the reason she doesn't think we should be spending time together, so I change the subject to something lighter.

We talk TV and books, then dip into politics. We circle around to movies, then she tells me about the one vacation she and Parker *did* take to Disney World a few years ago. Parker had always wanted to go—to Epcot rather than the Magic Kingdom even as a kid, which emphasizes what Gemma has already told me about her and makes me think I'd like her. I tell her about the time Sally and I took Landon when he was five, and somewhere along the way, I start thinking about what it would be like to go with her.

Visualizing a fucking family vacation? Really?

I can picture other vacations with her too, just the two of us. Those thoughts aren't as crazy, though. I've had beach days with knockouts that inspired the idea to flicker across my mind of maybe taking a trip with them, shucking the stress of work for a few days, seeing that tight little body in a dozen different bikinis, waking up and having my cock sucked in a tropical paradise. Never pulled the trigger, but I thought about it.

I've definitely never had a flicker of interest in bundling our families and going somewhere together, though. That's... not the kind of thing you do with someone unless you're pretty serious about them.

I try to shake it off, not least of all because if our kids really hate each other as much as she thinks they do, that's not something we could ever do.

I can see her point that them not getting along would be an obstacle, but I don't agree it's the absolute end of our chances together. Both of our kids are seniors in high school. They'll be off at college next year starting their own lives, and any contact between them after that would be minimal. Holidays, family events, but they wouldn't have to be around each other on a regular basis.

Christ, listen to me thinking about this like it's what I actually want.

It's not. After I lost Sally, I had no desire to attach to someone I might lose again.

I like Gemma, that's all.

It doesn't mean we have—or need to have—a future together. I'm just enjoying her company right now.

WHEN WE FINISH EATING, Hayden packs everything up while I play with Hades.

I haven't had a dog since I was a child and never a big, scary-looking one like this, but despite his menacing appearance, Hades is a sweetheart. He lets me rub his chest, then rolls on his back so I can give him a belly rub. He doesn't tolerate that for long before he's sitting up again, looking around the neighborhood like he's the king who reigns over it.

He's super cute, and I keep giving him pets and love until Hayden returns, grabbing my hips and tugging me back against him.

My blood warms as my butt connects with his body.

When I straighten, Hayden slides a hand under my shirt and rests it on my bare stomach. He caresses my skin beneath the tank top, making my heart pound and my body still against his. I look at him over my shoulder, my breath catching as he stares back at me with a smoldering glint in his eyes.

"I like this," he says simply. "Being here with you."

"I like it, too."

It feels like a shameful admission. An aching regret because the more I enjoy being around him, the more it's going to hurt when this is all over, and I can't be anymore.

Maybe we don't have many moments left, but we still have today.

God, I want to kiss him.

I want to turn around, wrap my arms around his neck, and press my lips to his. I want him to dominate my mouth like he did the other night, to drive out all my sensible thoughts until my legs are locked around his waist and he's carrying me in the house to do unspeakably dirty things to me.

Instead, I pull away and straighten my shirt.

He suggests we take Hades for a walk, so we do.

On our way past the Hartley house, no one is around, but on our way back home, Brent is outside with one of his sons. His face registers surprise when he sees us walking by with Hades, but Hayden doesn't even spare him a glance.

I do. I can't help it. I look back at him over my shoulder and barely resist the urge to call out, "Hey, neighbor!"

I'm feeling good when we get back to the house. Sweaty, though. It's a hot summer day, and Hades is panting after our walk, so I decide we should all go inside and drink some cold water.

I rinse out the bowl I gave Hades outside and get him fresh cold water from the compartment on my refrigerator. As I fill it, I smile and tell Hayden that when I was a little girl, I always thought you really made it when you had a refrigerator with an ice and water dispenser.

"Well, I guess you made it, then."

I'm taken off guard when he peels up the back of my tank top so everything below my bra is bare. He's dressed casually today in a white T-shirt and charcoal shorts with boat shoes, but I hear a rustling of fabric, and when he moves forward and wraps his arms around my waist, I feel his bare skin pressed to mine.

The contact of his hot skin against my back and the strength of his arms around me make my heart race with excitement. My body is already hot, and he's making it worse.

He kisses the ball of my shoulder, then takes Hades' water bowl from my hand. He has to put a little distance between us to bend and put it down for him.

I take advantage of the distance and turn around to face him, but as soon as Hades trots over to get a drink, Hayden starts moving toward me.

The counter is behind me, so I have no choice but to back toward my living room unless I want to be instantly trapped.

"What are you doing?" I ask, looking up at him. "I was going to get us a drink of water, too."

"I'm thirsty, but it's not water I'm craving."

He keeps coming, grabbing at the hem of my tank top and tugging it up over my head as we move. He tosses the shirt on the couch, then closes in on me.

I'm hot and sticky, and my thoughts are muddled.

I'm overpowered by him, intoxicated by his incredible, masculine scent.

I let him pin me against the back of the couch and trap my hands. I let him kiss me, his hard body pressed against mine.

I want to wrap my arms around his neck, but when I try to pull my hands from beneath his, he locks his hands around my wrists, holding me in place while his mouth ravages mine.

It strikes the same chord as the other night when he held me down on the bed and drove into me. He won't let me go anywhere. He *makes* me *let* him kiss me.

It's hot. Really, really hot.

When he finally releases my wrists, his greedy hands slide down my body. He grabs my ass and pulls my pelvis against his, but he inches closer so he's still forcing me back against the couch.

The way he has me trapped here, I can't move much. He slides his fingers into the waistband of my shorts and starts to push them down, but I can envision what happens if I let him.

He's going to fuck me right here, against the back of my couch.

I can't let him do that. I'll never be able to sit on it

again without remembering him bending me over it and pounding his cock into me.

"Hayden, no." I catch his hand and gently tug it away—or try to, but he doesn't relent.

"I want them off," he murmurs, kissing the underside of my jaw, then kissing his way down my neck.

"There's a zipper on the back, but I don't want you to take them off."

That's only half true.

But we can't, not here. Not on the couch I sit on with my daughter.

Like I didn't just ask him not to, he reaches back and grabs the zipper. He seems hell-bent on getting me out of my shorts, whether I'm game or not.

What will he do to me if he succeeds? *Will* he fuck me, or maybe just touch me? Maybe he'll press a finger into me and tease me until I come apart in his arms. Maybe he'll push me to my knees and free his cock, demanding relief after he's given me mine.

A torrent of naughty, sinful possibilities runs through my head.

I'm staring at his muscular chest as he holds me against him and drags down the zipper on the back of my shorts when I hear Hades' toenails on my hardwood floor.

I pull away from Hayden to look behind him.

Hades stands a few feet from us with a curious look on his face. His tail wags like he's waiting to be invited to the love-fest.

"Aw," I murmur, reaching back and pulling the zipper up on my shorts.

I'm not one to turn down puppy dog eyes, even if the dog in question looks like he eats human souls for breakfast.

"Hades wants some loving, too, don't you, boy?" I shove Hayden away and slip out of his embrace so I can crouch down and give Hades some attention.

Hayden sighs heavily, turning around to watch me give scratches and pets to his brother's dog. "You know, bringing the dog seemed like a good idea at the time."

Hades pants happily as I give him really good chest scratches.

Meanwhile, Hayden adjusts his cock and gives the dog a dry look as if to acknowledge my affection has been stolen away by a worthy rival.

"You're not so big and bad, are you?" I say sweetly, rubbing the dog's muscular body. "You're just a big lover boy, huh?"

"Never let my brother hear you talking to one of his fearsome beasts in that voice," Hayden says dryly.

Hades wags his tail and rests his big head on my shoulder. "He's not a beast," I say soothingly, shooting Hayden a look. "He's a sweetheart."

"He's a cockblock," Hayden states, but at least he's smiling wryly.

He *is* a bit of a cockblock, but I'm glad for it.

I was caught up in Hayden's irresistible sexiness, but I

hadn't *wanted* to have sex with him in my living room, and now that moment has passed, thanks to good ole Hades.

Since we're both hot and bothered, I tell Hayden I need to take a shower and clean up before we start the second part of our date.

He decides to use our short intermission to take Hades back home.

I'm a little sad to lose our chaperone.

Hades would have probably been more effective at keeping my clothes on than I'll be by myself, but realistically, I knew this night wouldn't end before Hayden and I had sex one last time.

I think about it as I dry off after my shower, then rub lotion all over my body.

I think about it when I pick out a pair of blue lacy panties to wear under my strapless midnight-blue sheath dress with a keyhole cut out between my breasts.

I love this dress.

The fabric is silky smooth against my skin, and it clings to every curve on my body. It's very sexy, so I grab a thin white cardigan to go over it, then I find a pair of navy blue flats to finish the look.

I'm not sure what we're doing for the next part of our date, but just in case a lot of walking is involved, I don't want to be wearing heels.

It's a few minutes before six when Hayden rings my doorbell.

"You changed," I say, leaning against the doorframe and looking him over. He's wearing a black button-down shirt with the sleeves rolled up to show off his sexy arms and a pair of dark blue jeans.

He looks me up and down, a faint smile on his perfect lips. "So did you," he points out. His gaze lingers on my bare legs, and I shift on my feet, anxious to get out of here before he gets me in the house and out of my clothes.

"Are you ready to go?" he asks.

I nod and grab my purse, then I make sure to lock up.

Parker should be home from Hannah's house soon, so I text her in the car to let her know I'm going out, and to text me when she's home and the place is locked up again.

I have to admit, though, I feel safer than I did before Hayden got involved. I know there are cameras, and I'll get an immediate notification on my phone if anything is amiss. I can check the live view anytime to make sure everything is all right, and now that the neighbors think Hades might be staying with me, I highly doubt any of them will step foot on my property.

He really has made all of my problems go away.

Well, those problems.

He's a whole new problem, and I have a feeling he won't help me fix that one.

HAYDEN TAKES me to a nice restaurant for dinner, then to his brother's bar for a couple of drinks.

I don't drink as much this time since I'm less nervous. When I feel myself getting tipsy, I switch to water, then when Hayden finishes his drink, he pays the bill, takes my hand, and we walk along the beach.

I love walking the beach at night. It's so peaceful.

I take off my flats and carry them in one hand so I can sink my toes in the sand.

Hayden hangs back and watches me for a little while. We don't talk, but the silence is companionable and not awkward at all. I love being around someone I can just be with in the quiet without the constant expectation of conversation. Some moments don't require words.

I move closer to the water's edge so I can use my toes to write in the wet sand before the water comes and washes it away.

That's our relationship, really. We're playing in the

sand, knowing the waves will wash it all away before anyone can ever see it. It'll be like it was never there to begin with, and only we will know it was.

It's kind of beautiful in a way.

It could be sad, but I'd rather think of it as beautiful.

The waves lap at my ankles. I wish I had a swimsuit on underneath my dress. It's a balmy night, perfect for playing in the water without worrying my fair complexion will earn me a painful sunburn.

Turning back to Hayden, I look him over. He's standing guard, his hands shoved in his pockets, watching me play in the ankle-deep water.

"Have you ever gone skinny-dipping?" I ask him.

His lips tug up. "Yes. Have you?"

I shake my head and make another heart in the sand while the waves roll away from the shoreline. "A friend dared me to once, but I was too afraid someone would see me."

"Is that a common occurrence for you?"

I look up at him, a questioning smile on my lips. "Do a lot of people dare me to skinny dip?" I tease. "No, I can't say they do."

He smiles but shakes his head, still wanting his answer. "Do you skip a lot of experiences because you're afraid of them?"

That wipes the smile off my face. "I'm not timid. I'm just practical. If the payout doesn't justify the risk, I probably won't do it."

"It just doesn't seem like you take many chances."

"I take chances when I think they're worth it. Opening my own dance studio was a big risk," I point out, though I'm not sure he knows I *own* the studio. He may just think I'm a teacher there, working for someone else. "I had to invest everything I had in that studio and just *hope* it would work out. It could have cost me everything if it hadn't. I wouldn't have been able to pay my bills or take care of Parker. We would've lost the house because I'm the sole earner and I wouldn't have been able to pay the mortgage. It was immensely scary, but I took the leap."

"Why?"

"Because..." I sigh, thinking back to that time. "Because I wanted more. I was unfulfilled in my other jobs. I'd worked several, but I wasn't passionate about any of them. I was just toiling away for a paycheck. I've had to make a lot of sacrifices over the years due to circumstances and bad decisions. I just decided life is too short to spend all of it doing something you don't love."

Hayden nods. "That's true. Life *is* short."

I nod and look down, etching a swirl in the sand at the water's edge. "That payoff was worth the risk, so I took it. Now, I make my living doing what I love, and I get to be my own boss. Parker dances, too, so I even bring her as my assistant when her schedule allows it. I wouldn't be able to spend that extra time with her if I still had any of the crappy jobs I worked before."

"It sounds like you construct your whole life around her. You and your daughter must be very close."

"We are." I'm hesitant to ask, but I'm also curious

about his relationship with his son. "Are you and Landon close?"

He doesn't answer right away. His gaze drifts to the ocean behind me. "We were once," he finally says. "A long time ago."

I step even more carefully here since I can tell his wife's death is still a source of pain for him. "When your wife was alive?"

He nods. "My whole life with her was only possible because she was who she was. To be honest, I'm not sure I was cut out for family life, but it was easy to fall into it with her. She made it easy. I loved our life together. Then she was gone, and all of a sudden, it was up to me. I was lost in my own grief, so I couldn't... I couldn't pull anyone else out of theirs."

Even from a distance, I can feel the pain radiating inside him. It bleeds out around him like a force field that should keep me away, but it pulls me in instead.

I feel no jealousy that he loved his wife so deeply, only sympathy because he lost someone who clearly meant the world to him.

I don't know if it's the right thing to do, but I can't stand here and watch him hurt without at least trying to help. I step out of the water and slowly approach him. My touch is tentative as I reach my arms around him, just in case my comfort isn't welcome, and he wants to push me away.

He doesn't. He doesn't return the hug, just stands there as solid as stone, but he lets me hug him. I press my head against his heart and listen to the strong thud of it beating in his chest.

Maybe I've been too hard on him about his son. Landon *is* a jerk, but they have both been through an unspeakable tragedy. Perhaps talking to him will work. Maybe he could even benefit from having a loving female influence in his life again. It doesn't sound like Hayden has really opened up to anyone since his wife died.

I'm not sure I could be that for him, though. I know I could if not for our conflict of interest, but my heart isn't big enough to wrap around anyone who is cruel to my daughter.

My heart is big enough to wrap around Hayden, though. I can feel it expanding and wrapping around him now, trying to absorb some of his pain so that at least he doesn't have to feel it all alone.

"Your wife sounds like an incredible woman," I say softly against his chest.

"She was." He grabs the back of my sweater and uses it to tug me back. I think he's pulling me away from him because he wants space at first, but then he wraps his hand around my neck, keeping me still so he can lean down to brush his lips against mine. "She would've liked you."

A smile tugs at my lips. That feels like a really solid compliment coming from him. "I bet I would've liked her, too."

My eyes drift shut as he kisses me. It's slow at first, following the pace set by the ocean lapping at the shore.

He kisses me, and his lips linger. He kisses me again, and just tastes my lips.

It's the most intimate thing I've ever experienced, and despite—maybe because of—the excruciating slowness, my heart pounds more and more furiously in my chest.

I ache for him. I could no more resist his deepening kiss than I could my next breath. When his other hand slides down and bunches up my dress, I pay no mind to whether or not we're still alone on the beach. His hot palm moves down my lower back, then pushes into the back of my panties so he can grab my bare ass.

Arousal pools between my thighs. Tightens when he slides his hand lower and grazes my pussy.

And just like that, I'm on my back in the sand with Hayden's body covering mine.

I run my hands over his handsome face so I can memorize the feel of his stubble against my fingers. If we only have tonight, I want to remember every minute.

I push my fingers into his hair as his greedy hands roam my body. My legs are wrapped around him, his hips grinding into my pussy, but it's not enough. I want him inside me.

I start unbuttoning his shirt, and he lifts up long enough to shrug out of it. He throws it on the beach and reaches for the button on his jeans.

I'm startled when I feel a vibration against my inner thigh. Is it coming from his pants pocket?

Did he bring... a toy?

Interesting.

Did it turn on by accident, or does he have a remote?

"Is that...? Um... your pocket's vibrating."

He frowns, ripping his phone out of his pocket and casting an impatient glance at the screen. He must not recognize the number or not think it's terribly important because he ignores the call and tosses the phone on the sand.

His attention shifts back to me, a wolfish smile on his handsome face. "Now, where were we?"

I grin as he leans in to kiss me, eager to pick up where we left off, but before we can get much further, his phone is ringing again.

"For fuck's sake," he says, rolling off me and grabbing the phone. He swipes the screen and puts the phone to his ear. "This had better be pretty goddamn important."

I study his face, but his urgent call reminds me that I haven't checked my phone since we came down to the beach.

Parker was supposed to text me when she got home from Hannah's house, but I hadn't heard from her last time I checked my phone.

If there's still nothing, I need to call her. Maybe she went home but forgot to text me.

My stomach drops when I pull out my phone and see a ton of missed notifications. There are missed phone calls and voicemails, the top text reading, "Where are you?" and a note underneath that I have twenty-three missed text messages.

And they're all from Parker.

"Oh, my god." My stomach plummets even lower. My fingers tremble as I swipe open the chain and scan the messages. There are so many.

The first message says she just got home from Hannah's house, and it was an hour ago. Shortly after, a text that says, "Is that you?" I keep scrolling, and the next messages are Parker saying she thinks someone is in the garage.

"Oh, my god. Hayden. Something happened. Something's wrong. I have to go home right away. Oh, my god," I say, my heart nearly giving out when I get to the one that reads, "Mom, I think there's someone in the house."

"Hayden," I scream, finally getting his attention.

He's still on the phone, but he looks at me, wide-eyed.

"We have to go. Something's wrong, something happened. Parker—I missed a million messages from her. My god, I should have been home."

Helpless tears spring to my eyes. I haven't even finished reading the texts. Illogically, I'm too afraid to. Too afraid of what they'll say. I don't even know if she's okay.

"I'm going to *kill* them," I growl, choking on sobs at the same time. "Please, we have to go now."

Hayden must see how panicked I am as I push up off the beach and shakily get to my feet. He stands, too, but he's not in enough of a hurry.

My leg muscles have melted again, making it hard to move quickly, but I'll crawl to the car if I have to. "Please, hurry, we have to go."

"Gemma." He grabs my arm to steady me, but I try to shrug him off so I can run up the beach toward the car.

"We have to *go*. Parker thinks there's someone in the house. I have to—she called me. I need to call her back. We need to call the police."

He hasn't moved. He's still holding the phone in one hand, my arm in the other. "Gemma, calm down."

"Don't tell me to calm down! Let me go. My daughter needs me, and I'm not there!"

"Parker is fine," he promises.

"You don't know that."

"Yes, I do."

His voice is so calm while I'm so frantic. It takes a few seconds for that to register and for me to notice the grim look on his face.

Any other time, I would care enough to ask, but if Parker might be in danger, or if she was in danger before and I'm too late to help her, then nothing else matters. Nothing else will ever matter.

"Please," I say tearfully. "I have to get to my daughter."

"Parker is okay," he assures me. "I'll take you to her right now."

"Why are you so calm?"

Dread darkens his features. He looks down, swallows, then looks back at me, but something is different. He no longer looks like a man confident anything in the world he wants will be his. He looks like... like he understands what I've known all along.

We are *impossible*.

My stomach rocks, but I don't understand why. My instincts click the pieces together before my tormented mind can. "Who was on the phone?"

"The first call was Landon."

"And the second?"

"A friend of mine at the station."

"The station?"

He closes his eyes and nods.

"The... police station?"

He nods again.

"Why?"

Hayden sighs softly, his eyes opening back up. I can see the regret and frustration. "Because Landon was arrested."

My eyes widen. "For... for what?"

"Breaking and entering."

MY RAGE CAN SCARCELY BE CONTAINED as I escort Gemma into the police station.

She has calmed down some since I filled her in on what I knew of the details. No one was hurt. My fucking son just had too much to drink with his asshole friends and thought it would be fun to give Parker Johansson a good scare.

Turns out, the cameras I had installed caught the asshole who has been playing juvenile pranks on Gemma and her daughter.

Also turns out, it wasn't her sleazy neighbor.

It was *my fucking son*.

Even if I would've pieced together that the pranks began the year he got his driver's license, I never would have guessed that.

All along, Gemma has been trying to tell me he's the immovable object in the way of us ever being together, and all along, I have thought she was overreacting.

I guess not.

Gemma hasn't said much to me since she wrapped her head around the fact that my son broke into her home tonight to go after her daughter. Most of the ride here was silent and not in the peaceful way it was earlier.

She doesn't know her way around the police station, so she has no choice but to stick close to me as I lead her to Parker.

She breaks away from me as soon as she spots her.

I've never seen Parker, but I recognize her immediately because she looks so much like her mother. The same big doe eyes and similar ginger hair, though hers is longer and not as bright as her mom's. She's sitting cross-legged on a chair in a pair of black yoga pants and a baggy gray sweatshirt, her long hair piled in a messy bun on top of her head.

"Honey," Gemma says, rushing to her side and pulling her daughter into her arms.

Parker returns her mom's hug, but her gaze meets mine as I walk past them toward the desk where my son is sitting.

Landon is wearing dark wash jeans and a black hoodie, his dark hair mussed and his face set in a sullen expression. It's clear he's resentful about being here, like it's not his own damn fault he is.

He doesn't look at me as I approach. He looks past me at Parker and her mom embracing.

"Didn't know there were two of them," he says in a glib, sarcastic tone that makes me grind my teeth.

"You think this is funny?" I ask him, stone-faced.

He shrugs and crosses his arms over his chest as he gazes up at me. "I got a good laugh out of it."

The police officer who called me as a professional courtesy is sitting at the messy desk, offering me an embarrassed, apologetic smile as my son shows his ass.

I desperately want to wring Landon's neck, but I can't blow up in public, so I shift my attention away from him.

I shake the officer's hand and thank him because we both know my son shouldn't be sitting here sulking in the police station. He should have been processed and had his ass thrown in a cell with all the other criminals.

The officer fills me in on what's happening and tells me—so Landon hears, since he's undoubtedly been a pain in the ass since he sat down—how lucky we are that this didn't turn out much worse. The homeowner could have had a gun and killed him. They could have had a guard dog and set them loose on the intruder.

I am belatedly thankful that I didn't leave Hades with her like I thought about doing because he's absolutely right. This could have gone *much* fucking worse.

The police officer goes on to tell me (and, incidentally, Landon) that breaking into someone's house is not a prank, it's a felony, and since he's eighteen years old, there's no choice but to try him as an adult.

I can hear the distant sound of his entire fucking future going down the toilet.

I squeeze the bridge of my nose, knowing beyond a

shadow of a fucking doubt that Landon hasn't just ruined my night.

He has completely ruined my chances with Gemma.

Or, maybe more accurately, he has forced *me* to ruin my own chances with Gemma, because as much as I like her, and as much as I know Landon was entirely in the wrong here, I also know there's not a shot in hell I'm going to let this happen.

I can't.

Landon might be an asshole, but he's still my son.

Sally's son.

It dawns on me that he's gotten so far away from me that I don't even recognize him anymore. This angry, sullen kid is not the little boy who joyfully flung water at his mom under a waterfall in Costa Rica. He's not who he was on track to grow up to be when she died, either.

He was left in my care, and I've failed miserably at my most important job.

His mother would never forgive me if she saw the mess I've let our son turn into.

It may be too late to change it now, but regardless, I have to do damage control.

I have enough of the right connections. I can pull the necessary strings to get him out of this.

But I can't do it without fucking Gemma over.

I don't expect it to sting as much as it does.

I don't know how a mere hour ago, I was clutching her tight and running my hands over her incredible body, and now…

Well, she'll probably never even speak to me again.

I pull the officer aside away from Landon so we can discuss in greater detail what needs to happen next.

The biggest problem is the statement Parker gave. He shouldn't show it to me, but he does anyway, and she describes in explicit detail that even though Landon came in through a garage door that wasn't locked, she called out a warning to leave and even told him she would call the police if he didn't. When Landon ignored her and proceeded to bang on her locked bedroom door demanding entrance, she shut herself in her closet "in fear for her life" and called for help. Landon proceeded to try to enter her bedroom, and it wasn't until officers showed up and dragged him out in handcuffs that Landon finally exited the home.

"Christ," I say, handing back the report.

The officer nods his agreement. "It's pretty bad."

I know he thinks my son's an asshole, but he doesn't say so. He probably also knows my son should see some jail time for how he behaved, but he knows this town well enough to know that's not on the table.

"If we can throw this statement out, it'll be much easier to make this all go away. But if the girl is persistent... it's going to be really difficult not to press charges. It can be done, but not as easily, and it won't be pretty."

I nod my understanding. I know exactly how they go about discrediting a woman's statement, and there's no way I can do that to Gemma's daughter. "I'll talk to her."

He goes back to babysit my son while I ignore the lead

balloon of dread in my gut and approach Gemma and Parker. They're not hugging anymore, but Gemma is sitting on the chair next to her daughter, her pretty legs turned in Parker's direction, holding her hand and nodding at something Parker is saying.

Gemma's wounded gaze drifts to me when I enter her line of sight.

Noticing she's lost her mother's attention, Parker turns to look at me, too.

This is certainly not how I wanted us to meet.

Not that it matters now.

"Are you all right?" I ask Parker.

Gemma wraps her arm around Parker's shoulders and pulls her daughter close as if to protect her from me.

And given what I'm here for, she's probably right to.

"She's understandably shaken up after what she went through tonight," Gemma states, her tone cool.

I nod, letting my feelings drain out of me. It's the only way I can proceed with shattering any lingering interest Gemma might have in me. "Landon is very sorry for what he did," I tell Parker.

Gemma snaps before Parker even has a chance to respond. "If Landon is very sorry, why isn't *Landon* the one apologizing?"

Parker responds before I can. "Because he's *not* sorry." Not broking bullshit, she meets my gaze dead-on. "I don't know if you think I'm some utter fucking moron or what, but I know your son isn't sorry. And I know you're probably saying he is because you want me to rescind my statement and say something like, 'oh, I was confused and thought he was an intruder, but we're actually friends from school, and I just didn't expect him to stop by,' so I'll save you some time. Not a chance in hell. Your son *trapped me* in my bedroom tonight and tried to break down the door. God knows what would have happened if he would've succeeded."

I open my mouth to speak, but before I can, Landon calls out from across the room. "Bullshit. If I wanted to break down your fucking door, I would have. I was only trying to scare you."

Parker lifts her eyebrows and gestures to Landon. "See? He's not sorry. And I'm not taking back my statement. I have put up with *a lot* from your son over the years. If this is how it finally ends, so be it."

Wow. Parker is not what I was expecting after having met her mother, but it's hard to argue any of her points—at least, when she's the one I'm arguing with. Sure, I could dig around her life and find grounds to discredit her in the court of public opinion if I had to, but I don't want to. I like Parker, and I like her mother, and none of this is their fault.

My gaze shifts to Gemma, holding her daughter like a protective mama bear.

Even though Parker is the one who has been through a trauma tonight, her hand rests over her mother's kneecap like she's providing her stability and comfort, too.

And I'll bet she is.

Gemma is an absolute sweetheart, but her protective—

and more assertive—instincts come out when she needs to protect her daughter.

I bet the daughter is just as protective of the mother.

I'm a bastard to use personal information Gemma has given me when we've spent time together, but she said herself that Parker is mature for her age, that it has always been just the two of them.

Ordinarily, I'd want to speak with a parent over their child, but I have a feeling Parker can handle herself.

"May I speak with you alone for a moment?"

Parker's eyebrows rise in surprise.

"I don't think that's a good idea," Gemma says.

Parker's eyes narrow but never leave my face. She's debating, and she must decide she's not afraid to go toe-to-toe with me because she moves her hand off her mom's knee, gently moves out of her embrace, and stands. "No, I'll talk to him."

I offer her a mild smile. Not that she seems to need the reassurance, but I don't want her to think of me as the bad guy here.

Ridiculous that I'm still trying to salvage things when I know the chances of Gemma ever looking past this are fucking minuscule.

Since this area is so open that anyone can overhear, I find an empty interrogation room I can use to converse with Parker. Gemma does not like that at all, but Parker assures her mom she's fine and follows me in.

I close the door and gesture for her to take a seat.

She shakes her head knowingly, crossing her arms. "I'm okay to stand."

I nod slowly, trying to get my bearings. I'm at a disadvantage not knowing this girl. I've had minor interactions with females Landon has brought around, but none of them have been as capable as I take Parker to be.

"Your mother tells me that you and my son have had run-ins for quite some time."

"My mother?" she echoes, her eyebrows rising.

I know Gemma hasn't told her she's been spending time with me, so I say, "She came to my office the other day about your neighbor. We ended up discussing your relationship with my son."

Parker nods, her lips pressed together. "Ah. Well, I don't have a relationship with your son any more than the mole and the mallet have a relationship in a game of Whack-A-Mole."

"I understand that you probably hate him and want to see him punished," I begin.

"I don't hate him. I mean, I don't *like* him, but that's not the problem. He hates *me*. That's the problem. I don't have to do anything to provoke his bullshit. In fact, in the past, I have been really nice to him. Now I try to stay in my lane and mind my own business, but it doesn't get him off my back. He's the one who won't stop harassing *me*. It is not a mutual problem we have. I never did anything to cross Landon. He just zeroed in on me like a psycho because I tried to be nice to him one time, and no amount of demanding *or* begging him to leave me alone since has worked. Your son has issues, and I don't think jail is the place for him to get the help he needs, but you know what? Maybe it is."

I bow my head, reevaluating my approach based on this new information. I expected a scared, belligerent teenage girl hell-bent on vengeance.

This girl is not angry.

She is calm and reasonable, and again, I cannot help liking her.

Sighing, I meet her gaze. "I'm going to be very honest with you, Parker, because I respect you. I'm going to talk to you like an adult because I think you deserve that, and I think you can handle it."

She doesn't say anything, just stands there with her arms crossed and her poker face in place.

"There is not a reality in which my son goes to jail for what he did tonight. That is not to say it wasn't wrong. It was. Unfortunately, the world doesn't work that way. Justice isn't always black and white, and the court systems do not always provide it. I promise you that if you fight this battle, you will lose. It's not your fault. You are simply outmatched. I do not relish that fact. I am not trying to embarrass you or hurt you. I'm just giving you the reality of this situation. You can stand your ground and refuse to budge from the truth, but Landon will not go to jail, and I urge you to remember you still have to endure senior year with him. If my son is as horrible to you as you say he is, can you imagine how much worse it will be if you try to defeat him and *fail?*"

Parker swallows, a glint of vulnerability in her eyes.

I can see that she does.

She doesn't admit it out loud, but I know she's piecing together that if Landon gets away with his bullshit and emerges unscathed, he will think he is invincible.

And he won't be grateful for his good fortune and stop tempting fate—he will come at her even harder.

"Wouldn't it be so much better if he believed that *you* decided not to pursue this?" I suggest.

Parker's gaze drops. I see her mulling over her limited options. Her gaze shifts back to mine, and she looks much younger, like the vulnerable teenage girl she actually is. It makes me feel like a fucking monster for manipulating her.

"I'm not a combative person," she tells me, shaking her head. "I don't *like* any of this. But he came to my *home*. I don't care what he said out there. I believe he wanted to hurt me. I think he would have if he could've gotten past my door."

"I understand," I say with sympathy I don't have to manufacture. "And you can rest assured I will deal with my son's behavior. I'm not asking you to let him hurt you or not to stand up for yourself. Whatever it takes, I will make this right with you and your mother. I just want to do it outside of the legal system. I was going to offer to pay off your house as a thank you if you'd let this go, but if you really want to steer clear of my son, I'll purchase you guys a different home in a different school district and you can finish your senior year elsewhere. I know your mother doesn't love the neighbors in your current neighborhood, anyway. She might welcome a change of scenery."

She surprises me by shaking her head. "I'm not going to let him chase me out. I've worked hard for my accomplishments at the school I've spent my entire high school career at. I don't want to go somewhere else."

"All right," I say easily. "It was just an idea."

She eyes me distrustfully. "You'd really pay off my mom's house?"

I nod. "Absolutely."

"I'd want it in writing," she warns me.

I can't help grinning. "All right."

Her eyes narrow with suspicion. "What?"

I shake my head. "Nothing. I just like you, that's all."

My answer surprises her.

"Not in the alarming way my son seems to," I specify. "I just think if I had a daughter, I'd be happy if she were like you."

I expect some part of that might make her cheeks redden, but I'm surprised when she flushes and what she seems to focus on is the first part. "Landon does *not* like me."

That's not worth arguing about right now, so I nod as if I believe her and extend my hand in her direction. "Do we have a deal, then?"

She stares at my hand for a long moment, then she says, "I want something else."

I lower my hand. "What's that?"

"I need—" She stops and clears her throat. "I need a

new laptop for school this year. Mom's been trying to find the extra money to buy me one, but—"

I don't make her finish. "Done. I'll give you my email address. Send me the link to whichever one you want, and I'll have it delivered to your house."

She looks relieved. I see more of her mom in her as she softens and gives me a little smile. "Thank you."

I WAS twelve years old when I broke the nasty habit of nail biting, but as I wait outside the interrogation room at the police station, I'm tempted to start up again.

After what feels like an eternity, the door finally opens.

Hayden holds the door for Parker, and she brushes past him to return to my side.

I eye her up, searching for any visible sign of distress. "Are you all right?"

Arms crossed, she nods.

It strikes me as a self-protective gesture, though, so I'm not so sure. I look back at Hayden, my eyes narrowed. "What did you need to discuss with my daughter by herself?"

"It's fine, Mom," she says before he can say anything. "He wasn't mean to me or anything. We just talked, and he apologized." She glances over her shoulder at Landon, who is still watching her like a little creep.

I grab her shoulders and pull her in front of me. "We need to go."

Parker nods her head but says she needs to talk to the police officer about one more thing she forgot on her report before we leave. I offer to go with her, but she doesn't want me to.

I don't like her even approaching the officer since Landon is sitting right there, but the officer seems to understand they need to be separated, so he directs her to follow him into a nearby office.

Now that my daughter is out of the room, my attention returns to Landon.

He must feel my gaze on him because while he was still looking at the door Parker walked through, now he looks back at me and looks me directly in the eye.

I glare at him so he feels bad, but he doesn't.

He smiles and gives me a little wave.

Ugh, he's such a jerk.

Looking back at Hayden, I cross my arms and say, "Now do you see the problem?"

He nods, and I can see that he does. "I didn't realize how serious it was."

"I tried to tell you."

"I know you did."

Since he's not arguing with me, I don't know what else to say.

I look down, noticing the granules of sand stuck to my feet since I put my shoes back on in such a hurry.

The memory surfaces of my arms wrapped around him, his lips on mine. How much I wanted him...

The waves lapped at the shore too soon. Our picture got erased before we could even finish drawing it.

Without anger and fear, I just feel a little sad.

I really did like him, it just doesn't matter.

It's like I said from the beginning—there's no future for us together. It's just not possible.

"I don't know if I'll need a lawyer to handle this stuff with Landon, but obviously, if I do, it can't be you. Since I'll probably have to hire someone more in my price range, I'll just have them deal with my neighbor stuff if it's a problem going forward. I'm not even sure what my neighbor was responsible for and what Landon did. Maybe my neighbor is just a creepy sexist and not responsible for any of the other stuff."

"I'll talk to Landon and find out," he assures me. "I'll let you know."

I nod. "Thanks. Beyond that, I don't think we should talk anymore."

He doesn't look surprised. He nods, but it doesn't feel like agreement, just an acknowledgment of my preferences.

I'm too tired to insist on clarification.

It has been the longest, most terrifying night of my life, and all I want to do is go home and curl up in bed with my daughter, where I can rest assured that she is safe and sound and within my reach.

Parker emerges from the office and makes her way to

me with her head down, probably to avoid catching Landon's gaze again. I escort her out of the building as quickly as possible so we can put all this behind us.

When we get outside, I realize I'll have to drive her car home since I don't have mine.

Parker seems to realize it, too, when she gets in the passenger seat and frowns thoughtfully at the door leading into the police station.

She looks over at me, her brow furrowed in confusion. "Did you and Landon's dad get here at the same time?"

I don't have the energy left to lie to her tonight. It feels pointless to have made it this far without her knowing and then have to come clean, but I'm on the verge of mental exhaustion and just don't have it in me.

"I was with him when he got the call that Landon had been arrested. I checked my phone and realized I'd missed all those calls and texts from you. It was because I was with him."

Understandably, she looks confused. "But... why? Where were you?"

"At the beach," I say softly, starting up the car and mustering what's left of my energy to drive us home.

When we pull into the driveway, it feels like the scene of a crime.

I guess because it is.

There's dust residue on the doorknob from where they collected his fingerprints. When I walk into the kitchen, I can't help knowing someone else was in this room while I was out—someone who meant to do my daughter harm.

When I walk up the stairs, it's impossible not to wonder what it was like for her. Did she run up these same stairs, terrified, with him on her heels? Is she reliving all of it as she walks through our home?

Parker doesn't balk when I tell her I want her to sleep in my room tonight. It's been years since she crawled into my bed to go to sleep, but there's no way I would be able to sleep with her anywhere else.

As tired as I am, I can't seem to fall asleep even with her right next to me. I lie in bed with my eyes burning and my emotional stores entirely depleted. I'm desperate to sleep but surprised by the overwhelming emptiness I feel.

I know it's just because I'm exhausted. I'll feel better after a good night's sleep.

The dark room lights up, and I glance over at my phone on the bedside table.

I look over to make sure Parker is still asleep, and when I see that she is, I grab my phone.

It's a text message from Hayden that simply says, "It was all him and his friends."

"Were they here tonight? Why aren't they in trouble, too?"

"They bailed on him," he texts back. "They were game to spook her but not to come inside the house. When he went in the house, they drove away so they didn't get in trouble, too."

"Some friends," I text.

"Yeah."

Our conversation is at its natural end, but for some

reason, I don't want to put down the phone. I feel comfort just looking at the screen and seeing his words.

The phone dims while I look at it, but then it brightens again, and I see three bubbles on his side to indicate he's typing.

"I'm sorry we didn't get to finish our date," he says.

"So am I," I type back, but it makes me feel sad.

"I really want to see you again."

I sniffle and type back, "No. I'm sorry."

"I understand," he says.

This feels more like a breakup than my last *actual* breakup did. I want to keep talking to him so I don't feel so heartbroken, but I know it's just delaying the inevitable.

I type out *Good night, Hayden,* but then I backspace it and send a message that reads, "Goodbye, Hayden."

I wait for him to answer that one, but he doesn't.

The screen dims, and still I wait.

I don't want him to say goodbye back, but part of me does because I need to know he understands I really mean it this time.

Before, it may have been hard to resist him. I said no and knew I *needed* to mean it, but this time, it's different. This time, I *mean it* mean it.

I wait, and I wait.

I fall asleep with my phone in my hands.

But he never texts back.

LIFE GETS BACK to normal in the days that follow.

I'm off work for two weeks between summer recitals and the start of my fall classes. I always schedule it that way so Parker and I can spend a lot of time together before she goes back to school, knock out any shopping that needs to be done, cram in a few last late nights of staying up watching movies or bad TV shows we won't have time for once school starts.

Parker notices I'm staying in every night and assures me that I don't have to. "I'm fine," she insists. "I'll keep the door locked. I bought a Taser. I don't want you to be afraid to go out and live your life just because I go to school with a lunatic."

I smile faintly. "I'm not afraid," I tell her, but that's a bald-faced lie.

She doesn't have a child, so she can't understand the helpless terror I felt that night when I saw those missed messages. Before I knew the entirety of what had happened, and the absolute worst-case scenarios were playing out in my imagination. When I thought for a horrifying moment that I was being felt up on the beach by a man whose son may have been hurting my daughter, or even worse.

I don't know Landon Atwater. I don't know what he's capable of.

"You just..." Parker starts, but trails off unhappily before she can finish.

I glance over at her. "I just what?"

She shrugs, looking at me. "You seemed happy."

Tears sting behind my eyes all of a sudden, but it must be my period coming on because there's no way I'm getting emotional over this.

I force a smile and grab a Twizzler. I tell her I *am* happy, and she lets it go, but I can tell it's still on her mind.

I'm so reluctant to leave her home alone that I put off grocery shopping until Friday. We're out of food to make dinner, and Parker wants to spice it up with chicken tikka for dinner tonight, so I have to make a supply run.

I make my rounds as quickly as I can, and when I return home, Parker is at the table playing around on her laptop. She seems extra cheerful, and I wonder why, but when I ask, she just smiles, closes the computer, and helps me put the groceries away so we can get started on the prep for tonight's dinner.

"By the way," she says as she prepares the marinade for the chicken, "I got an email from the school. You need to go to some emerald parent meeting this weekend."

"At the school?"

She shakes her head. "Of course not. You know the parents at my school, they're bougie. It's on someone's yacht. I'm sure there will be Dom and salmon puffs or whatever rich people eat."

I crack a smile. "I don't want to go to a yacht party without you. Can you come?"

"Nope, parents only. It's some 'strategy meeting.' I guess they're strategizing how to get the school year off to a great start or something. I don't know, I'm sure it'll be lame, but you have to go. It's mandatory."

"What does one wear to a mandatory yacht party?" I question.

"Something cute." She flashes me a smile. "I'd wear a bikini underneath, just in case."

The sun is mere minutes from setting as I walk along the dock, looking for the yacht where Parker told me this meeting was happening.

"Poseidon," I murmur, spotting the trident symbol and nodding. "There it is."

I expected other parents would be waiting by the boat, but I am running a few minutes late. I had to make sure the house was locked up before I left, and even once I was sure, I checked again.

Parker has bounced back from the night Landon broke in much faster than I have. She acts like I'm overreacting to still be so worried, but I still feel immense anxiety when I have to leave her alone at the house.

I don't keep my phone on vibrate when I'm away from her anymore, and I know I can check the cameras Hayden had installed anytime, but the fear is still there.

"Hello?" I call out, searching the boat for people, but I don't see anybody.

It's a pretty big boat, though. Maybe everyone else is inside.

I feel strange boarding someone's boat without their explicit permission, but I check the information Parker gave me again, and this is definitely where I'm supposed to be.

"Hello?" I call out again hesitantly as I enter the cabin.

I've never been on one of these luxury yachts before, but I'm shocked when I enter the room, and it's like a lavish living room. Three couches occupy the center of the room with windows to view the ocean on either side. The whole room is decked out in black and brown. Definitely big enough for a bougie meeting, but I still don't see any other parents.

Beyond the living room is a gleaming dining room table with a tin bucket full of orchids at the center.

I feel nosy, but I look around the cabin and even travel up the stairs to the next level. The bedrooms have walk-in closets and gorgeous bathrooms with Jacuzzi tubs. There's even an office. It's literally like a house on the water, but I can't find any people in it.

I make my way back to the lower level, but I realize the boat has pulled away from the dock as I pass a window.

My stomach drops, even though I guess it's understandable that if the meeting is happening on a boat, we're probably going for a ride.

I'd feel a lot better about knowing I'm out at sea if I could find other people and be sure I'm where I'm supposed to be.

I head to the back of the boat so I can see how far we've made it. Not that it matters. It's not like I can jump off and swim back.

I mean, I guess I could, but...

This is supposed to be a mandatory meeting.

I'm about two seconds away from texting Parker when I *feel* his presence behind me.

I turn, and my heart leaps with relief and some other, less acceptable thing I decide not to put a name to.

Hayden stands there in a pair of white shorts and a light-blue button-down. His handsome face is a sight for sore eyes. I have to resist the urge to walk up and touch him just to make sure he's really here.

Because he shouldn't be.

Kids at Parker's school are divided up by house. Parker's house is emerald, and she said this meeting was for emerald parents.

Hayden's son is onyx.

"What are you doing here?" I ask him, afraid I already know the answer.

"Finishing our date."

I glance back over my shoulder. Naturally, there's more space between us and the dock than before.

I look back at Hayden and sigh. "There's no school meeting, is there?"

He shakes his head.

"You sent my daughter a fraudulent email to lure me here under false pretenses? I'm no expert, but you are—isn't that a crime?"

He smiles faintly. "I didn't send her a fraudulent email. Parker knows where you are. She knows you're with me. She helped me set it up."

That throws me for a loop. "What—Why would she do that?"

Feigning—*but is he, really?*—smugness, he says, "I guess you were miserable without me."

I roll my eyes. "Ugh, I was *not*."

He moves closer, reaching out and grabbing my waist so he can pull me in. "No?" he murmurs, dipping his head and kissing me. "I was pretty miserable without you."

I can't resist kissing him back, but I pull away before he can pull me under and obliterate my senses completely. "I told you I didn't want to see you again."

"You did, but it was a lie. Anyway, you owed me the rest of that date, and I'm not a man who lets his debts go uncollected."

I pull away from his embrace with some effort. "Hayden, I'm serious. We talked about this. You saw what Landon did..."

"My son is not dangerous," he says seriously. "I know

he did an idiotic thing and scared you half to death. I understand that, and I'm very sorry. The truth is..." His jaw locks, and he looks out at the water. Whatever he was going to say, he doesn't finish. He looks back at me and says, "He knows that he can't pull a stunt like that again. He's out if he does."

"Out?"

"Of the house. Of his trust fund. Everything he holds dear is gone if he comes after Parker again."

"Oh," I murmur, surprised to hear that.

"He's grounded and not allowed to hang out with his bonehead friends for a while. I have his car keys, and he's effectively under house arrest for the remainder of the summer, so I promise you don't have to worry about Parker."

Easier said than done.

"Parker is worried about *you*," he says.

"Because I'm wasting away with want for you?" I ask sarcastically.

He cracks a smile. "No. Because you've put your life on hold for her, and she doesn't want you to wake up one day when she's off at college and realize you're all alone and you don't want to be. Now, I'm not saying I'm your destiny. I don't want to argue with you about the kids or the impossibility of our future together. I just want to enjoy the rest of the date you promised me. That's all."

I'm not sure I believe him, but I'm not sure I have much of a choice, either.

I bite down on my bottom lip, glancing back at the dock one last time.

"For the record, this feels a lot like kidnapping," I tell him.

He takes my hand and pulls me up the stairs. "That's a good note. Do you *not* like dates that include kidnapping?"

"They're not my favorite," I inform him.

"I'll keep that in mind for future reference." He looks back at me over his shoulder. "See? We're getting to know each other better already."

I shake my head at him but fail to bite back a smile completely.

If asked, I would have definitely said no to this "makeup date," but I can't deny I feel a little happier now that I'm here.

When we get to the top deck, he hauls me past the hot tub and around the dinner table. I notice this table is set for two, but he moves me past it to what I can only possibly describe as a bed. I guess it's a lounge area, but it has pillows everywhere and a soft-looking blanket draped across the bottom. It may as well be a bed, just one out in the open beneath a canopy of stars.

Well, it will be set beneath a canopy of stars soon.

The sun hasn't set just yet, and I realize that's why he brought me up here.

Two yellow and orange drinks wait for us when we settle in, and a cold bottle of water for me.

"My two drinks," I say, smiling.

"When it comes to beverages, you like to keep your options open. I remembered."

I can't help grinning as I drop to my butt on the comfy lounge area. "You did." I grab the glass nearest my water and take a sip. "Mm, that's delicious."

"I'm glad you're finding the sustenance at this meeting satisfactory."

I scoff. "Meeting."

"It is. A *strategy* meeting," he stresses.

"Mm-hmm. And what, pray tell, are we strategizing?"

Hayden reaches forward and grabs his drink, then leans back against the pillows and takes his time looking me over. "Currently, I'm strategizing how best to remove your panties. Conventionally, with my hands? Maybe I should tear them off with my teeth instead."

"That is *not* the strategy meeting I signed up for."

I lean over and put my drink up on a ledge so I don't melt all the slushy ice with my body heat. As I do, Hayden grabs me and tugs me over closer to him.

I don't balk when he pulls me so I'm lying half on top of him.

It feels really nice, actually.

I settle my arm around his waist and my head on his bicep.

"I love watching the sunset," I tell him quietly.

He sighs with contentment, so I guess he does, too.

AFTER WE ENJOY THE SUNSET, I hear movement on the deck behind us, but Hayden isn't alarmed and tells me it's just the chef setting up dinner.

Since I know we'll be eating soon, I finish my fruity cocktail. To be honest, I'm sad when it's gone, and I wish I had more. It was *so* good.

Maybe a little too good. I trip over my own feet when I stand up.

"Some dancer I am," I joke, a little embarrassed by my lack of grace.

Hayden grabs my hips to stabilize me and teases me, calling me a lightweight.

"You probably drugged me or something," I mutter, only half-joking. "Can't ship captains marry people? If I wake up married tomorrow, I'm gonna be *so* mad at you."

Hayden snort-laughs and follows me to the table. "You shouldn't give me any ideas."

"I'm so serious about this," I say, pointing at him as I

drop gracelessly into the booth side of the table, then scoot down to where the food is. "I am not getting married without Parker."

"You're thinking an awful lot about marriage for someone who refuses to date me," he says reasonably, but entirely unconcerned by the tipsy woman talking about tricky weddings on his ridiculous super yacht.

"I need to eat something," I tell him. "I didn't eat much today, and either you drugged me, or that was a very strong drink."

"Well," he says casually as he unrolls his silverware. "I've already been accused of kidnapping and fraud today. I suppose we may as well add drugging you to my rap sheet."

I shake my head in mock disappointment. "Some lawyer you are."

Once I have some food in my belly, I don't feel as tipsy as I did before, but I still feel happy. I hate to admit it—actually *loathe* to admit it—but I think it's just because I'm spending time with Hayden when I thought I never would again.

The chef clears our empty plates away, and Hayden thanks her. When she's finished cleaning up, she goes below deck to give us some privacy.

"So," I say, gazing at him across the table. "You've been emailing my daughter?"

He nods unapologetically, like that's a perfectly natural thing to do. "Since the night we met. She's a smart kid. I like her."

"Yeah, I'm pretty fond of her myself."

He cracks a smile. "I noticed. She's pretty fond of you, too."

"What... um, what do you talk about?"

"Lots of things. Mostly, we started out talking about you. She wanted to know what had been going on between us and why we were at the beach that night. What we were *doing* at the beach."

"You better not have told her that."

He smirks. "I kept it PG, but I think she's smart enough to read between the lines. She was surprised and said you don't usually get serious with guys very fast, but she could tell you really liked whoever you were sneaking out with."

I cover my face with my hands. "God. That makes *me* sound like the teenager."

"When I told her you didn't think we could really give dating a chance because she and Landon didn't like each other, I think she felt bad."

My amusement fades, and I uncover my face. "You shouldn't have told her that."

"Why? It's the truth."

"I know, but it's not her problem. I don't want her to feel bad about it."

"After that, we started talking about other things. I think she wanted to get to know me a little bit, see if she approved."

"Did she?" I ask lightly.

His eyes glint with amusement. "She helped me kidnap you, so she must have."

"What a traitor." I shake my head playfully but realize I haven't checked my phone in a while. I haven't heard it go off, but I want to make sure I don't miss anything.

I did. Just one text message from Parker.

"Having fun?" she asked.

I smile faintly and type back, "Yes. Thank you."

Since I didn't know I was getting kidnapped tonight, my phone doesn't have a full charge. I didn't realize how low my battery was, but looking at it now, I see the bar is in the red.

I don't want to risk my battery dying and Parker not being able to reach me again, so I ask Hayden if he has a charger on the boat that I can use.

He tells me he does and leads me down into the cabin I'm guessing would be his. It's the master suite, if a boat has such a thing—and this one does. There's a king-sized bed, but the bedroom is so big that there's also a little sitting area with a couch and a couple of end tables on the other side. There's a master bathroom with a shower and tub, and his and hers sinks on opposite sides of the room. The biggest walk-in closet is off this bedroom, and so is the office.

"I can't believe you have a study on your boat," I say, leaning forward to poke my head inside. "Parker would love this."

"It's pretty much a whole house," he verifies. "We lived on it for a year while our house was being built." He reaches for me, taking my hips and pulling me around to face him.

On instinct, I wrap my arms around his neck and gaze up at him. "You *lived* here?"

"For a time. I used to love the ocean. Felt more at home out here than I did on land."

"What happened?" I ask, though I think I have an idea. Maybe it's better if he tells me himself.

Hayden sighs, his arms settling around my waist. His gaze shifts away from my face, but his grip seems to tighten. "Six years ago, I was at work on a Saturday. I wasn't supposed to be. It was my day off, and I guarded those pretty fiercely back then. I wanted to spend all the time at home that I possibly could. Like you, I wanted to soak up all the moments."

I smile faintly when his gaze flickers back to mine, but he averts it just as fast.

"But on this particular Saturday, I decided to go in. Wanted to impress the partners with my dedication to the case. We'd been planning to take the boat out that day. I told Sally we'd do it Sunday instead, but Landon was determined to go out on that boat, he didn't want to wait. Sally decided there was no reason they couldn't go out without me. We loved to boat, so we could go out again Sunday if we felt like it. It wasn't even unusual for them to take the boat out without me, they did it all the time. So, they did it that day. And like a hundred other times before, they jumped off the boat and swam around in the ocean.

They were both strong swimmers, so they liked to splash around and have fun."

He pauses, his gaze drifting to the window. I know the ocean is out there, but right now the water isn't peaceful and beautiful. It's dark and terrifying, an abyss you could easily get lost in.

"Landon was twelve. He was the only eyewitness, so it's impossible to fill in the gaps, but he said they were just swimming and playing in the water when suddenly he realized the only sounds he heard were his own. He turned around, thought she must have been waiting underwater to pop up and startle him, but he didn't see her anywhere. He swam around in circles, looking for her head in the water, looking for the shape of her body underneath. He looked up on the deck, thinking maybe she'd climbed back on the boat, but she wasn't there. She wasn't anywhere. He dove back in the water, and he dove, and he dove, and he dove. He screamed for her, and finally, one of the crew came to see what was going on." He shakes his head and looks straight at me. "The ocean betrayed me that day. It swallowed her up."

I caress his hard jaw, trying not to envision Landon as a desperate little boy searching for his mother when she was already gone.

"There's no closure with a death like that," he finally says. "The ocean is vast and full of predators. They never found her body. For days, weeks, months, I didn't want to believe it. Maybe she was out there somewhere. Maybe somehow, I'd get her back. But I knew it wasn't true. I could feel it in my bones. I brought the boat out time and time again trying to find her, but once I accepted that she was truly gone and I wasn't going to find her no matter how much I looked, I brought the boat in and never took it out again."

"I'm so sorry, Hayden," I whisper.

He meets my gaze. "For years, I've been haunted by the same dream. We're out on the boat, and she's alive and there with me, but something feels off. It feels like a mean trick, but I can't completely understand why until it happens. One minute, she's there on the deck with me, and we're just enjoying one last day together, and the next, she's jumping in the ocean. That's when it hits me. If she goes into the water, she'll never come back up, but it's too late. I call out to her, and I lunge, trying to catch her to pull her back up, but she disappears beneath the water. I can jump in, I can dive and dive like Landon did that day, but I can never get her back."

Something that sounds almost like fear can be heard in his voice. It's powerful and deeply rooted, and I wish I could scoop it out of him and throw *it* in the ocean.

His arms tighten around my waist, and he pulls me more snugly against him. "The other night, I had the dream again. I was out on the boat, which I hadn't been on in years. But this time, it wasn't Sally on the deck with me. It was you."

My heart sinks. "Me?"

He nods. "*We* were enjoying a day together, and it didn't feel off at all. I didn't even realize right away it was the same dream because this time, everything felt right. You were wearing sunglasses and a white cover-up over your bathing suit. But then you stood and took it all off. You asked me if I'd ever been skinny-dipping, and then you jumped in the water. And as soon as you hit the water, that panic came back. I remembered what was going to happen. I dove in after you, but I've had the dream so many times, I knew how it would end. The same way it always ends, with me desperately reaching for someone I can never hold again."

The way he says that cuts deep, and since I *can* hold him right now, I do.

I close my eyes and rest my head against his chest. My arms reach around his muscular back, and I hold him as tight as I can.

Then he speaks again. "But I was wrong. This time was different. I plunged my arms into the water, and I ripped you from the ocean's deadly clutches. You were wet, and you were scared, but you were there, and you were mine. I held you in my arms, and you held me right back, and... it was like the nightmare was finally letting me go. It was like I finally had a second chance." He leans in so his forehead is resting against mine. "You were my second chance, Gemma."

My eyes fill with tears because I want to be so badly.

But it was just a dream.

I can't say that to him, though. Not right now. Not after what he just shared.

Then his lips find mine, and I kiss him back with the

same desperate hunger.

When he lifts me and carries me back toward the bed, I'm as eager as he is to get there.

His hands are greedy and rough as they squeeze and caress my skin, running his hand over everything he can touch like he's taking stock of a prized possession. He puts me down right in front of the bed, catching the hem of my dress on the way down so he can grab my ass.

He lets go and searches for a zipper on the back of my dress. When he finds it, he drags it down and pulls the material forward.

He sits me on the edge of the bed and rips his shirt off without bothering to unbutton it. I'm wide-eyed as he pushes the material off his muscular arms and throws it on the floor, then even more turned on when he looms over me, his sun-kissed, muscled chest and abdomen on full display.

He's so beautiful.

I lick my lips and look up at him.

He reaches out and grazes my bottom lip with the blunt end of his thumb, then gets back to undressing me.

He drags down my dress, his mouth grazing every newly exposed inch of my body with a searing heat.

My god, I've never been touched like this before—even by him.

He's not kissing me, he's consuming me. I'll be ashes by the time he's done with me, but I'm too caught up to reach for a bucket of water to save myself.

He hoists me and yanks the dress away from my body,

then throws me back on the middle of the bed. I'm star-tled, but it quickly melts away when he comes down on top of me.

His weight feels strangely reassuring as he presses down on me. I rest my hands on his broad shoulders and kiss him back when he kisses me.

His mouth leaves a trail of wet kisses down my neck, my breasts, my stomach, and doesn't stop until he reaches the top of my panties. His greedy fingers hook into the front of the flimsy material, then he's dragging it down, following the path with his mouth and kissing his way down my thighs.

"I love the taste of you," he says hotly, pulling my panties off and tossing them on the floor.

"Hayden—" My voice breaks over his name.

Before I can say a thing else, his mouth latches onto my pussy, and I cry out, sinking my fingers into his hair.

He growls around my clit as he tongues it, and the vibrations shoot through me like a bolt of lightning.

I can't believe a man can make me feel this way. No man ever has before him. They've never even come close.

His fingers spread me open, then he angles his tongue against my clit. My hips arch off the bed as he begins to fuck me with his tongue, hitting that sensitive spot again and again at just the right speed. He's as relentless at this as he is everything else, so it's maybe a minute later when I feel the desperate elation of an orgasm that's about to hit.

"Hayden," I cry, throwing my head back against the bedding. "Oh, god."

And then I'm coming on his face, crying out in ecstasy and twisting helplessly as pleasure courses through my body.

I lie boneless against the mattress as he rises up and looks down at me. He looks gorgeous looming over me, like a god surveying his kingdom.

He shoves off his shorts and his underwear, and palms his cock as he gets ready for me.

I know he's going to fuck me now, but I'm too blissed out to even move.

He climbs over me and grabs my hands, pressing them into the mattress above my head. I sigh at the feel of his muscular length against me. At the insistent hardness of his cock resting against my thigh.

"Kiss me," he commands.

I can barely move, but I find the strength to lift up and press my lips to his. His lips taste like paradise, and his tight grip on my hands makes me feel like his prisoner.

The combination is intoxicating.

He shoves into me without warning, making me gasp and jerk my hands, trying to break free. He doesn't release me.

He grips my wrists with one hand to keep them over my head and lets his other hand slide down my arm, down my naked body until his palm covers my breast, kneading the soft flesh and tweaking my nipple as his cock moves deeper until he's filling me all the way.

It's the best feeling in the world to be so full of him. I can feel him stretching me in all the right ways, feel the slow build of tension deep inside as he finds a rhythm and starts to move faster and faster.

My tits jiggle as he drives into me, and the sight makes him growl and bend to kiss them while he's fucking me. His mouth on my flesh intensifies my building pleasure, and I know he's going to make me come again.

If he keeps giving me these double orgasms, he might make some headway on this dating business. I didn't even know that was a real thing that happened, but I am a big fan.

I arch up off the bed so I can get closer to his lips, needing to taste him as he pounds into me. When our lips connect, it's like a match lighting a fuse. I explode like a rocket, crying out as he wraps his arms around me and holds me tight against his body. I grab his shoulders and melt against him, moaning and whimpering as his cock pounding into me extends the spark of my orgasm.

"Christ," he groans, squeezing me close and burying his face in my neck as he drives deep into my convulsing pussy and comes inside me.

We collapse against the bed—sticky, sweaty, and completely sated.

His big hand comes up to brush my hair out of my face. He can't seem to resist absently kissing my lips while he's there.

I'm feeling too many amazing things to process, so I wrap my arms around him and get as close to him as I can.

"I love your cock," I murmur.

A startled laugh slips out of him. "Yeah?"

"Mm-hmm. I'll marry it. You, I'm not sure about, but—"

He cuts me off, tickling me mercilessly rather than letting me finish that sentence.

"Okay, okay," I cry, pushing his hands off me and laughing. "I give up."

He smiles, kissing me, then yanks me against his side.

We may both be hot and sweaty, but I'm happy to be here. I rest my head on his chest and enjoy the feeling of being held in his arms. It reminds me of the dream he had, the one where I replaced his wife, but he got to *keep me*.

I wish you could.

The impossible dream whispers across my mind, threatening to dampen the mood, but I don't let it.

I close my eyes and shove it away.

I soak up the moment because I know it can't last.

CHAPTER 15
HAYDEN

I CAN'T REMEMBER the last time I watched a sunrise.

Holding Gemma in my arms, witnessing her simple pleasure as she sighs and leans back against me, watching the light in the sky shift as the sun comes up...

I shouldn't like it so much, but I do.

If I could start every goddamn day this way, I think I would.

I don't have a damn thing to complain about today.

When I woke up in the middle of the night, Gemma was wrapped in my arms. We showered together in my bathroom. She was feeling generous, so she sank to her knees, took my cock in her lovely little mouth, and showed me a slice of heaven I hadn't experienced with her yet.

I pushed her up against the shower wall, slid my hand between her thighs, and fingered her until she came too, then we stood under the hot spray with our arms around each other for the longest time.

Now, we're out here watching the sun rise with chilled champagne and a bowl of fresh strawberries.

Gemma leans back against my chest and opens her mouth.

I grab a fresh strawberry from the bowl and hold it to her lips.

I watch as her teeth sink into its juicy flesh and her lips wrap around it.

My cock stirs as she licks the juices off her lips and welcomes my hungry kiss when I can't take it anymore and need to feel her underneath me.

I hold her in my arms, and she wraps her legs around my hips. I fuck her again as the sun moves higher and higher in the sky.

Afterward, we lie sated in each other's arms.

Like I said, a perfect fucking morning.

I kiss her tit as she lies there gazing up at nothing—not to start anything again, just because she's close, and I can't *not* kiss her when I have a chance.

I shouldn't even be able to want her again, but it's like that first night.

Every taste makes me hungrier for her.

I've experienced lust plenty of times, certainly enough to know that's not what this is. It's something different. Something deeper.

Something that's going to make the next year of my life nearly unbearable if she continues to insist on not dating me.

And she will. Gemma might be soft and malleable in

some ways, but she's also the sneakiest kind of stubborn. She's got it in her head that she needs to spend this year with Parker, and I've got it in *my* head that she needs to spend the year with me.

There's only one way to get both of us what we want, and I'm going to have to lawyer my ass off to make it happen.

"I've been thinking about Parker and Landon, our situation with them."

Gemma looks up at me.

"I think the best thing to do is deal with it head-on. Yeah, we can spend this year keeping them apart, but that's not a solid permanent solution."

"It isn't?"

I shake my head. "See, I'm gonna marry you, and I know you'll want Parker back here every chance you get once she goes off to college. It's unlikely that I'll be able to keep Landon away for all of those same occurrences. Not impossible, and if it comes to that, then it comes to that, but obviously, that is not how I *want* the future to unfold."

"You're saying a lot of things."

I pretend not to know which part she objects to. "What? You don't want Parker to come home all the time?"

She rolls her eyes. "I'm not marrying you."

"Yes, you are. We just discussed it last night, remember."

"You're confused. I said I'd marry your cock, not *you*."

"I'm afraid we're a package deal."

She wrinkles her nose up as if disappointed. "Aw, really?"

I crack a smile and look out at the water. "Anyway, once we're married, Landon and Parker will have to see each other from time to time. It's all but inevitable. Parker also seems willing to make peace with Landon for the sake of our relationship as long as he's willing to do the same."

"You've spoken with her about this?"

"I have. I wanted to feel her out, see if he'd eaten away at all of her goodwill or if there was a chance we could broker peace between them." I glance down at her, noting her lack of enthusiasm for my plan. "I understand that she's your daughter, and you're protective of her. I'll be protective of her, too, I promise. But Landon is my son. Flawed though he may be, I still love him. I won't allow his bad behavior to endanger your daughter, but if we can all come to an understanding, I think that would be a lot better."

Gemma sighs. "Don't you think it's a little late for that? I mean, with the cops and the arrest..."

I'm not eager to share this tidbit. "About that..."

Her gaze shifts to mine warily. "What?"

"Parker took back her statement."

Gemma's brown eyes widen, fury sparking in them as she clutches the blanket against her bare chest and sits up. "What?"

"We can all agree that Landon has to be dealt with. But this... this is a family matter, and I'd rather handle it personally than in the legal system. What he did was a felony, Gemma. I can't let my son start his life out as a felon."

She sucks in a breath, scooting away from me. "If he didn't want to start his life out as a felon, maybe he shouldn't have *committed a felony* against my daughter."

I knew she would be mad when I told her, but I'm glad it's out there now. "I'm not letting him get away with it. I'm just asking you to be open to the idea of forgiving him and moving past this if Parker can. I know he scared you, and I know you're still dealing with anxiety over all of it. I even know he's a jerk." I move up behind her, rubbing her tense shoulders as she looks out at the water to avoid looking at me. "But the kid's been through a lot. I'm not making excuses for him, but if I'm being honest, I haven't been the greatest father since Sally died. I want to make some changes in that area of my life. I want to get back to having an actual family, and I really want you and Parker to be part of it."

She looks back at me over her shoulder, her brow creased with wariness. "When you say family..."

I lock an arm around her neck and yank her back against my chest. "I can't believe this is the second time in my life I'm doing this without a ring, but I guess when it comes to forever, I'm incredibly impulsive. I want to marry you, Gemma. For real."

"That's insane. You're insane."

"Maybe," I murmur, still holding her against me. "I don't mean tomorrow or anything. We can have as long of an engagement as you want. A year, two years, five years. I don't care about the paperwork. I just want you close. I'd like for you and Parker to move in with us."

"What?" she says in a tone of disbelief, trying to pull out of my embrace, but that only makes me hold her more tightly. "Hayden..."

"I know it's fast, but I know what I want in the long run, and I don't want to be without you in the meantime. Life is short, and I don't want to spend another day without you in mine. I know it won't be smooth sailing, and we have big obstacles in our way, but I promise I will level all of them one way or another if you'll just be mine."

Since I won't let her go, she tips her head back to look up at me, her big brown eyes swimming with emotion. "Are you serious?"

"Completely."

She lets out a noise caught between a laugh and exasperation. "I won't even agree to *date you,* and you think we should get married?"

My lips tug up. "I think that's the answer. You said yourself, once you commit to someone, it takes a lot for you to come untethered. Commit to me. Then you'll try harder to get past this Landon stuff and make it work."

She sighs. "I don't know, Hayden. I mean... I obviously enjoy being with you, but... I just don't think Parker would be comfortable."

"All of this is pending Parker's approval."

She looks up at me uncertainly.

"Honest to God. If Parker doesn't want to do it, we don't have to. If you guys move in and we try to make it work with Landon, but we can't, I'll move him out and get him his own place for senior year to keep him away from her."

Her wide eyes meet mine. "You would move your own son out of your house?"

"If it's a matter of Parker's safety, of course. I love my son, so I'll do my best to resolve this in a different way, but if he's determined to be a dick, I won't indulge his bad attitude at the expense of Parker's safety or comfort. If it doesn't work with all of us living together, he can go. You have my word."

She stares at me for a moment, then she whispers, "This is crazy." But I can hear the excitement bubbling up in her voice and see it building up in the smile she's trying to bite back.

I lock my other arm around her, too, and bury my face in her neck. "Good crazy, though. We all win this way. You can spend all the time you want with Parker and all the time you want with me. Hell, if you want to, you and Parker can plan the wedding. I'd marry you tomorrow. The engagement timeline is completely up to you. I don't need any time to consider it. My mind's made up. I've seen what's out there, and I choose you."

I KNOW HE'S CRAZY.

Right?

Yes, definitely crazy.

But...

No, he's entirely crazy. I just like what he's selling, so I want to entertain it.

At least I'm honest enough with myself to admit it, I guess.

There's no way we're ready to get married, but he's kind of right. Being engaged isn't an irrevocable step. People get engaged all the time. Hell, *I've* been engaged once, and it didn't end in marriage.

And the guy sucked, unlike this one.

If it doesn't work out, it doesn't work out, but... what if it does?

Besides, it's like he said—none of this happens without Parker's blessing.

Parker's sensible, so she'll probably think it's

completely crazy. There's every chance she'll overrule it so I don't have to.

"I haven't lived with a man in a long time," I murmur in the car on the way home.

We're in my car this time, but I'm so distracted by Hayden's crazy plan that I forget to tense up when we drive past the Hartley's.

Not that I have to anymore, I guess.

If all goes according to Hayden's plan, I won't even *be* their neighbor anymore.

"I don't want to sell my house yet," I say suddenly, looking over at him as I slow down in front of my driveway. "What if it doesn't work out and I want to move back in?"

"That's fine," he says. "But if it doesn't work out and you've already sold your house, I'll just buy you a new one. It's not a big deal."

I stare at him as he says that like he's buying me a new dress instead of a *home*, but I also know that—knowing Hayden—failure isn't really an option. It's what he's telling me to ease my mind and ease me into it, but if he's convinced this is going to work, he'll make it happen, whether the world wants him to or not.

I let him come into the house with me and take note when Parker pops her head up from the book she's reading and flashes us both smiles. "Hey, lovebirds. Did you have a nice time?"

She seems comfortable with him, and that speaks

volumes. I didn't even introduce them. Hayden went out of his way to establish a relationship with her himself.

He has a pushy, single-minded way of doing things sometimes, but it's hard to deny it works.

"We did." I glance back at Hayden. I already told him in the car that I wanted to have this conversation with Parker myself. I don't want her to feel pressured, and she'll feel the least pressure if it's just the two of us. "Can I talk to you for a minute?"

Her brow furrows at my tentative tone. She nods, sliding the bookmark in her book, and follows me up the stairs.

We go to my room, and I close the door for privacy. I take a seat on the edge of the mattress and try to think how best to attack this.

If I'm being honest, I've never even considered having to tell Parker a thing like this. When things didn't work out with her dad, I sort of closed my mind to having serious relationships with anyone else, and no one came along to *change* my mind.

Until Hayden.

"Is everything okay?" Parker asks, sitting down beside me.

I look over and offer her a reassuring smile. "Yeah. Everything's good. I just... I have some surprising news, and I'm not sure how to tell you."

"Just spill," she says, watching me carefully. "You're not pregnant, are you?"

"What?" My eyes widen. "No. God, no."

"Phew. Then go on, tell me. Are you dating Hayden?" she teases, bumping her shoulder into mine. "It's fine if you are, Mom. I know you like him, and he clearly likes you. I want you to be happy, and if he makes you happy, then who cares who his son is?"

"Yeah?"

She nods confidently. "For sure."

"Okay." I fidget with the hem of yesterday's dress. "I guess that makes this a little easier to get out. It's still crazy, though, so prepare yourself."

She smiles. "I'm ready."

"Hayden asked me to marry him."

Her smile falls. "What?"

My smile turns apologetic and a little unsure. "Surprise?"

"I... wasn't ready." Her eyes are wide, and she shakes her head. "I don't understand. What's the rush?"

"We won't get married right away," I assure her. "He proposed, but it was impulsive. He didn't even have a ring. I guess that's how he proposed to his first wife, too. Once Hayden makes his mind up to do something, he just does it, to hell with proper form."

"Okay... So you're engaged but not getting married."

"Well, I mean, he wants to get married eventually. He's just not in any rush to the altar. But he is hoping we'll move in with him. With them," I correct, my heart flipping over in its cavity.

"Them," she echoes woodenly.

"But we don't have to," I tell her quickly. "We don't

have to do any of this. Nothing has to change. We can do senior year right here, just like we planned. If you're not comfortable with it, I'll wait. From the beginning, I told him he'll have to take a rain check if he wants to go out with me and wait until next year. We can still do that if you're not comfortable with this."

"I'm not going to tell you not to get engaged, Mom. I just..." She looks down at her lap. "I mean, you know how it is with Landon. How could we possibly live in the same house?"

"Well, I haven't seen it yet, but I have it on good authority it's a pretty big house."

The corner of her mouth tugs up at my attempt at levity, but my stomach knots up because she isn't comfortable.

"We—we don't have to do it if you don't want to. We *won't*. I don't want to if you don't want to. But if it changes anything, Hayden swears that if Landon acts up and won't get along with you, if he makes you feel uncomfortable or unsafe living there, he'll make him move out."

Her eyes widen to approximately the size of saucers. "He'll kick Landon out of his own house?"

I nod. "Obviously, he doesn't want to, but if Landon can't behave himself, yes. Yes, he will." I watch her face as she grapples with that new piece of information. "Really, it gives you power over him instead of the other way around."

"He won't like that," she mutters.

"I don't know if he knows the precise terms. We can

talk to Hayden more about it for clarification, but… that's the reality. Hayden wants us to resolve this and move on if we can, but your comfort is our utmost priority."

I sit there with her and go over all the facts until she's made a decision we both feel comfortable with. I know it's probably unconventional going to my teenage daughter for approval on my engagement instead of the other way around, but I don't care how other people do things.

Hayden isn't in the living room or the kitchen when we come back downstairs.

I start to panic that maybe he came to his senses and left, but we find him sitting on the front porch, watching the Hartley house.

Parker and I join him. Brent is piling luggage into the back seat of his car, and Lisa's standing in the driveway yelling something about custody.

"What's going on over there?" Parker asks tentatively.

"I forgot to call off my dog," Hayden says simply. He shrugs, apparently not too concerned about it. "Oh, well. He might not have littered your lawn with condoms, but he still behaved inappropriately toward you in the garage."

It's my turn to smirk. "Now who has to put a quarter in the inappropriate jar?"

Hayden rolls his eyes good-naturedly, but he's more focused on finding out how our talk went than pocket change. "Any news?"

I nod solemnly, then walk over and sit down on his lap.

He lifts my legs and drapes them over his, then links his arms together around my waist. "Good news?"

I sigh heavily. Keeping my face as serious as I can, I tell him, "It looks like you're stuck with me."

A grin splits his handsome face, and he looks at Parker for confirmation. "Yeah?"

Parker smiles. "I guess you're engaged. And we won't talk about how crazy that is, so... congratulations. I guess you get me for a daughter, after all."

I glance back at Parker, my gaze questioning.

She rolls her eyes good-naturedly. "Just something he said to me when we talked at the police station."

"Well, I am a man who goes after what he wants," Hayden says deviously, leaning in to kiss me.

"You sure are," I say, wrapping my arms around his neck and kissing him back. I'm cognizant of my teenage daughter awkwardly standing by, so I try not to linger too long, but I can feel Hayden's happiness, and I'm already bursting with my own.

It's crazy how this *feels* right.

"Why don't I take you ladies out to dinner tonight to celebrate?"

I'm about to say that sounds great, but much to my surprise, Parker chimes in with, "Shouldn't we include Landon in the big... official family celebration?"

"If he wants to come, of course," Hayden says. "I think I'll probably go home and share the good news with him myself, and then I'll pick you girls up after."

"Or we could meet you there," I suggest. "We haven't *seen* your house. I don't even know your address, and we're supposed to be moving in."

"That's true," he acknowledges. "Yeah, that's fine. You can meet me there, and after dinner, I'll take you in and show you around."

For my engagement dinner, I pick a cream-colored dress out of my closet. The knee-length gown with spaghetti straps is modest and simple, and perfect for a family dinner.

Family dinner.

With Landon Atwater.

It'll take some getting used to, that's for sure.

I assume Hayden wanted to tell him alone because he knows Landon won't consider our engagement such great news.

I try not to let it bother me, though. If I'm going to be his stepmother, I will have to try to bond with him, but the only way that will happen is if he starts being nicer to my daughter.

I know it will probably take some time. I try to tamp down my protective instincts and be patient.

I meet Parker in the hall. Her long hair is down, and she's wearing an airy red summer dress with a matching pair of red strappy sandals.

"Ooh, you look pretty," I tell her.

"Stop," she says lightly, looking me over. "You look gorgeous. Hayden is a lucky man."

We head downstairs to my car, and I put in the

address to Hayden's house. "I think what's crazier than being engaged right now is that I agreed to move into a house I've never seen," I tell her as we drive down to the edge of the road.

I don't even notice this time when we drive by the Hartley house.

Not that Brent is in it. He and Lisa had a big, loud argument in the driveway earlier. Something about how he could have fun with his hooker, so presumably she caught him cheating.

Hayden didn't offer any details, but he seemed at least a little bit responsible.

I'd feel worse about it, but Brent is gross. Whatever he may have done to instigate things, it's not Hayden's fault if Brent can't keep his dick in his pants.

We have to drive all the way to the beach to get to Hayden's house. I don't know the neighborhood at all, but I go where my phone tells me.

Even though I knew Hayden had money—*and a lot of it*—when the GPS tells me I've arrived at my destination, I can't quite believe it.

The sprawling hillside mansion in front of me is somehow not what I expected.

"Whoa," Parker says, echoing my thoughts as I roll tentatively into the driveway. "This is where we're going to live?"

It's white and black, three levels that I can see. The bottom level has windows of onyx glass like I might picture in a super villain's lair. The main level has a balcony that wraps around the sides and the back of the house. The top level sits proudly against the backdrop of a darkening sky, and while the purples and swirls of pink are beautiful, somehow the sight strikes an ominous chord.

It doesn't look homey, that's for sure.

Then again, home isn't a building with four walls and a ceiling. A house is what a family makes it, no matter how cold and imposing the structure.

"I like it," I say decisively, so my mind will fall in line.

This is our opinion. We like it.

Parker nods, but she doesn't say anything for a minute. "Should we go in?" she finally asks.

"I don't think so. Let's wait and see if he comes out."

We only have to wait a moment more before Hayden walks out the front door, looking incredible in a black suit with gleaming loafers. Parker and I get out of our car and I push the lock button on my key fob, then we climb into Hayden's Maserati.

He starts up the car without mentioning Landon, so I assume that means he's not coming.

Parker doesn't assume; she asks.

"Is Landon coming with us?"

"Uh, no," Hayden says. "I think he needs a little more time."

She sighs and looks at the house. "He should come. If we're going to do this, we should do it right."

"Well, I would have liked that as well, but it was his choice, and he'd rather stay home."

"Do you want me to try?" she asks.

I open my mouth to say no, but Hayden shrugs. "If you want to. He's in the living room."

"Why don't I go with you?" I say, putting my hand on the door latch.

"No," Parker says before I can open the door. "I'll just be a minute."

Tension gathers in my shoulders as I watch Parker walk up the staircase to the front door. Hayden reaches over and rubs them a bit, like he can tell the tension is gathering there.

"I don't like her being in there alone with him," I state.

"We've gotta let them work it out on their own. They're going to live together, Gemma. They'll be together in the same vicinity from time to time."

Not alone, not like this.

It's too soon. It stirs too many memories of that night and her frantic calls for help.

"Maybe this is a bad idea," I say quietly. "Not the engagement, but the moving in. I'm down to be engaged, but... maybe since we're taking the engagement slow anyway, we should pump the brakes a little. My house isn't the mansion yours is, obviously, but it's perfectly fine. You could stay there with us as often as you like if your goal is to spend time together."

I'm crawling out of my skin waiting for her to walk back out that front door.

"It will be fine," Hayden says with a calm I don't understand.

"She said she'd only be a minute. This feels like longer. I think I should go in there."

He squeezes my shoulder, partially to knead out tension, partially to keep me from getting out of the car. "Don't. Just let her handle it."

"He broke into our house to get to her, Hayden."

"He was drunk. He wasn't in his right mind. I assure you, he's completely sober right now."

I give it another minute, but when Parker still hasn't returned, I shrug his hand off. "I'm going in there."

I get the car door open, but as soon as I do, Parker comes back out.

Relief envelops me as I sink back into the seat. Her long hair blows in the wind as she makes her way down the steps.

I notice the troublesome kid from the police station isn't following her.

The back door opens, and Parker slides in.

I wait for her to close her door, then I look back. "No luck?"

She shakes her head. "No, not this time."

"Well, we'll have fun just the three of us," Hayden says, checking the rearview and then backing out of his driveway.

Turning back around, I ask, "Was he at least nice?"

"He was Landon," she says, which translates to no. "But give it time. I'm sure he'll come around."

"Yeah." Hayden says it like he agrees, but just yesterday, he was telling me he wasn't trying to convince me he was my destiny, and today, he proposed marriage.

Sometimes you have to consider the source when a lawyer's talking.

Hayden glances over at me as he puts the car in drive and starts to pull away from his house. "What are you smirking about?"

"Nothing. Just dogging your profession in my mind."

His eyebrows rise at the cheerful way I say it, then he laughs and grabs my hand, bringing it to his lips so he can kiss it.

His eyes shift back to the road, but it's somehow sweeter when he says casually, "I can't wait to spend the rest of my life with you."

I want to be as sure as he is that we will.

I'm not, but I *hope* we will.

Maybe I'm only less sure because Landon *is* his son, and Hayden might not like the reality as much as his promise. If Landon won't stop being a jerk and nothing we do seems to help, will he really kick his own son out?

It's hard to believe.

I know that even if Parker were a jerk to someone who moved in, there's no way I'd ever tell her to leave.

Hopefully, it doesn't come to that.

It doesn't seem like we're off to a good start, but I suppose if Hayden and Parker can be optimistic, then I can, too.

. . .

See more of Hayden and Gemma in Parker and Landon's book, *Contempt*, releasing summer 2022!

Turn the page for an exclusive look at Parker's last interaction with Landon, where she tried to convince him to come to the family dinner...

BONUS SCENE
PARKER

"I'll just be a minute."

I can tell Mom is worried as she watches me through the car window like a scared kid whose mother just dropped them off for the first day of kindergarten.

Hayden looks less concerned, but he doesn't seem to have a great deal of confidence that I'll change Landon's mind when he couldn't.

I take a deep breath as I make my way up the stairs and approach the front door. It feels odd to let myself in, but it would feel stranger to ring the doorbell and wait for Landon to answer.

Since I'll be living here now, I guess I can let myself in.

The door opens to a massive foyer with a staircase off to the right. A huge spherical waterfall chandelier hangs from the vaulted ceiling clear down to the railing.

The place is modern and cavernous, and not at all cozy.

The walls are dark, and the house is quiet. I know

Landon is alone inside, and I can't shake the ominous vibe as I walk tentatively down the hall toward the next open space.

It's a wide-open space with a staircase to the left and a stylish fireplace up ahead.

That must be the living room, where Hayden said Landon was.

Three steps lead down into the sunken space, and three gray couches are set up with a coffee table in the center.

My heart jumps when I see Landon sitting on the end of one couch, his dark gaze locked on me.

Fighting the impulse to turn around and avoid him—what I would ordinarily do if I ran into Landon in the halls at school—I tip my chin up and walk down the three steps so I can join him on his level.

He cocks his head, watching me curiously.

This is the first time I've had to see him since he broke into my house. It feels insane to be in his with him alone voluntarily, but I remind myself why I'm here and dig right in.

"Your dad said you didn't want to come to the club with us for dinner."

"Thought you'd be relieved," he says.

I look down. "I know we've had our differences, but they're really excited to celebrate their engagement," I tell him. "It's our first official 'family dinner,'" I say with air quotes and a faint smile. "We should all be there."

"No, thanks."

"It won't be the whole family without you."

"Don't care."

I try again. "I think your dad would really appreciate it if you came."

He gazes at me like I must be an idiot. "Is there something wrong with your hearing, or...?"

"I just... I feel like it's not really that much effort to come to dinner with us, and it would mean a lot to them."

"I don't care," he drawls, as if addressing the particularly stupid.

I pause. "You don't think you're being a little selfish?"

He smirks. "Trust me, you'll all have more fun without me."

"Don't do that." I sigh, dropping my gaze to gather my thoughts, then looking back up at him. "Look, I know this isn't... ideal."

"You can say that again."

"And I know that in the past, we haven't exactly been friends. I know you hate me, and I don't even know why, but it doesn't matter, honestly. Let's look at this as a fresh start. Whatever I did to offend you or infuriate you, whatever I did to make you feel the way you do about me, I'm sorry. Okay? But this isn't about us. Our parents are engaged now. I know it's crazy, and maybe you haven't seen them together yet, but your dad and my mom *really* like each other. I think they could be really happy together, and I would hate for *us* to stand in the way of that."

He nods slowly like he's mulling over my words.

Maybe I'm not as smart as I think I am because I feel an actual spark of hope that he'll be a decent human being and see reason for once in his life.

Then he opens his mouth and douses it. "And why should I give a single fuck about their happiness?"

My eyebrows rise and fall. "Um... I don't really know how to answer that. They're our parents. Don't you want them to be happy?"

He shrugs. "Their happiness isn't my responsibility."

Shoving down the surge of irritation he's triggering, I state, "No one is saying it's your responsibility, Landon, but they can't live together and be happy together if you and I can't find a way to get along."

He shrugs again, more deliberately. "Not my problem."

"Actually, it kind of is." I really wanted to be nice to him when I walked in here, but he's being such an infuriating asshole that my patience snaps. "We're moving in here whether you like it or not. And they're going to be happy whether you like it or not. I personally refuse to let you ruin this good thing they have going with your bullshit. If you want to be an ass and sit here alone by yourself instead of coming out to dinner with us, that's your choice, but I think it's a really shitty one."

"Has it ever occurred to you that maybe I don't want to *be* a part of your stupid family? Maybe I don't want to play house with my dad's latest lay."

I stiffen. "My mom is a great person, Landon. She will love you if you let her. I have already said I'm willing to put aside our differences and start over. This is happening whether we like it or not. There's no reason it has to be so contentious."

"No reason, huh?"

He stands, and I unconsciously take a step back.

He smirks and walks closer.

I fight the instinct to back away again. I don't want him to come any closer, but he clearly knows that, which is why he is.

I still think he's the most aggravating human on the planet, but when he closes in on me like this, I lose my grip on all my valid reasons for wanting to bitch at him and find myself fighting just to stand my ground. "I don't want things to be like this between us, Landon."

"I'm hearing a lot about what you want, Parker," he says slowly, stopping in front of me. "What about what I want?"

I don't like being this close to him. I shift my weight and subtly take a step back—not retreating, just moving so I don't feel as cornered. "What do you want?" I ask him.

"I want you and your gold-digging mother to stay the fuck out of my life," he says simply.

My hands clench into fists at my sides. "My mom is not a gold digger. You don't know her yet, but when you get to know her, you will see she couldn't care less about your dad's money. It's your dad she likes."

"Yeah, sure it is."

"It is, Landon." I look up at him, giving up my annoyance and softening since I know he's too much of an asshole to ever back down if I'm determined to butt heads. "Come to dinner with us," I implore, my tone a little cajoling. "It's just dinner. You have to eat, don't you?"

He holds my gaze for a moment wordlessly, then he lets me watch as his drops, moving slowly over my body and lingering in the most offensive places. My spine stiffens, and I look away. I know he's just trying to make me uncomfortable. I don't want him to see how well it's working, but I can't seem to help it.

Once he's raked over every inch of my body, his gaze returns to mine, a glint of dark amusement in his eyes. "You want me to come to dinner with you?"

It's a trap, I can feel it. "Yes," I say, anyway.

"Say please."

I suck in a breath at the demand, but it's not the words at this moment that steal my breath away.

It's when he said them before, the night he broke into my house.

When I was hysterical, sobbing on one side of my bedroom door with him on the other side, threatening to break it down.

Threatening much worse when he got inside.

Stop, I begged, crying.

Say please, he taunted, dragging his fingers down the door.

I didn't say please, and he didn't stop.

I hid in my closet and called the cops, and the few minutes it took them to get there and drag him out of my house were the longest and most terrifying of my entire life.

I'm frozen in place by the unpleasant memory, distracted enough that when I look up and he's right on top of me, my heart sinks with fear.

He grabs my chin, his touch deceptively gentle, lighting up every nerve ending he grazes. His blunt fingertip touches the seam of my lips, then he presses on the bottom one, parting them and forcing the tip of his finger into my mouth.

I turn my head to break his hold on me, hating the taste of him on my lips.

"Stop it, Landon," I whisper.

His tone is unyielding, remorseless. "I'm waiting for you to say the magic word."

I didn't say it that night, and I don't want to say it now, but I know it's my pride stopping me. The same thing that's stopping *him* from getting in that car and going to dinner with us.

I guess I can't ask him to let go of his if I'm not willing to part with mine.

We have to compromise if we want to get through this year living under the same roof. We won't make it if neither of us is willing to bend.

It kills me because he's being *such* a jerk, but I force myself to look up at him and give him what he wants. "Please come to dinner with us."

He smiles, but it's not a nice smile.

He reaches out and touches my lips again, this time grabbing my neck with his other hand so I can't pull away.

My breath catches.

"I changed my mind," he murmurs, watching my face.

I don't want his hands on me, but his grip only tightens when I try to pull away.

I force myself to relax, to just appreciate the ground I've gained and not fight him. He'll let go in a second, and then we can leave. Once we're in the car, we won't be alone together again, and he can't do shit like this in front of our parents.

"You'll come to dinner with us?"

He shakes his head. "Not about that. I think I'm going to like living with you."

His confidence makes my stomach sink.

"See, at school, you avoid me as much as you can. You request classes I'm not in like a fucking coward. I only see you around on occasion. But now? You'll be in my territory all the time. You'll sleep under my roof, right down the hall from me."

His words suck the breath from my lungs and plant seeds of fear in my heart.

His gaze drops. He's standing so close to me, holding my neck, I know he can see right down the front of my dress.

"Nice dress," he murmurs. "Nice tits, too."

"Let me go," I say, blinking first and breaking away from him. I can't stand his hands on me. I can't stand the words he's saying, or the way he's looking at me.

I can't stand the thought of sleeping in this house knowing he's down the hall.

For a terrible moment, I can't escape the fear and dread he makes me feel, and all I want is to be away from it forever.

This will never work.

But it has to work.

My mom deserves to be happy, and I know his dad makes her happy. I've seen it for myself, and she has sacrificed so much for me over the years.

Landon chuckles as I turn and hurry up the steps to get away from him.

"You still want me to come to dinner?"

I shudder, not dignifying his taunt with a response.

He can starve for all I care.

I sprint through the foyer and rip open the front door. A gust of warm air hits me as soon as I step outside and brings me back down.

I have to collect myself before I get back in the car.

My gaze flickers to the windshield. I can't see her from here, but I'm sure my mom is watching even now.

I force myself to chill out, pushing Landon out of my mind because he doesn't matter right now. I don't know how I'll deal with living with him, but I'm determined not to let him ruin any part of this, including our first dinner as a family.

I open the back door and slide inside.

The door is barely closed before Mom turns around in her seat, looking back at me anxiously. "No luck?"

I shake my head as I pull the seat belt across my lap. "No, not this time."

"Well, we'll have fun just the three of us," Hayden says, checking the rearview mirror.

Probably more.

I hate that Landon was right, but if I had convinced him to come, he probably would have made the whole night suck.

Turning back around, Mom asks, "Was he at least nice?"

"He was Landon," I say dryly. "But give it time. I'm sure he'll come around."

It doesn't feel like the truth, and it doesn't feel like she believes me, but she lets it go for now. I look out the window at the big, lonely mansion as Hayden backs out of the driveway.

I can't imagine ever thinking of this place as home.

I can't imagine feeling safe here with Landon under the same roof.

I also don't want his dad to make him leave. Maybe he'd deserve it, but it doesn't feel right.

I don't know how any of us will get what we want out of this.

Mom's smile steals my attention. I watch Hayden grab her hand and bring it to his lips to kiss it. They look so in love, and then he says, "I can't wait to spend the rest of my life with you."

My heart contracts.

I know my mom better than he does, and I know that

even if she wants that more than anything in the world, if she knew how Landon just acted toward me in the house, there's no way it would ever happen.

No way it *will* ever happen.

She'd never ask me to live here if she knew how much it would cost me, but I can't let her give up her happily ever after just because Landon's a jerk.

He might not care if they're happy, but I do.

Unfortunately, he knows that now.

I just told him.

Shit.

Sighing softly so Mom doesn't hear, I lean my head back against the seat.

I may not know how we'll all manage to live together, but I know one thing for sure.

Senior year is going to suck.

The story continues in **Contempt**!

If you haven't read **Even if it Hurts** yet, make sure you read that one before *Contempt*, too! Characters and storylines from this book and that one will pop back up in Parker and Landon's book. :)

Contemporary romance standalones

Untouchable (dark bully romance)

Descent (dark billionaire romance)

The Boy on the Bridge (second chance bully romance)

The Imperfections (forbidden romance)

Stitches (MFM ménage romance)

How the Hitman Stole Christmas (unconventional, a pinch of mafia)

Mistletoe Kisses (student-teacher romance novella)

Coming-of-age, contemporary bully duet

Because of You

After You

Forbidden, taboo romance

Irreparable Duet

If you're a **series reader**, be sure to check out her super binge-able Morelli family series! It's dark and twisty mafia romance, and the first book is *Accidental Witness*

The **Coastal Elite** world continues with *Contempt*. If you haven't read ***Even if it Hurts*** yet, make sure you do! After that, you'll be all caught up and ready for ***Contempt***!

ABOUT THE AUTHOR

Sam Mariano has a soft spot for the bad guys (in fiction, anyway). She loves to write edgy, twisty reads with complicated characters you're left thinking about long after you turn the last page. Her favorite thing about indie publishing is the ability to play by your own rules! If she isn't reading one of the thousands of books on her to-read list, writing her next book, or hanging out with her fabulous daughter... actually, that's about all she has time for these days.

Feel free to find Sam on Facebook (Sam Mariano's General Reader Group), Goodreads, Instagram, or her blog—she loves hearing from readers! She's also available on TikTok now @sammarianobooks, and you can sign up for her totally-not-spammy newsletter HERE

If you have the time and inclination to leave a review, however short or long, she would greatly appreciate it! :)